LARK UNDERGROUND

A Freddie Lark Mystery

ALEXANDRA AMOR

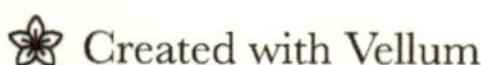 Created with Vellum

LARK
UNDERGROUND

For Greg and Steve (and Mango!)

Chapter 1

"Why are you doing this yourself?" she asked.

"Because I am a strong, independent woman," I said.

"And you're cheap."

"I am not cheap. I am resourceful. Besides, throwing money at a problem doesn't always get it solved properly. Hand me the channel lock."

"What's a channel lock?"

I was kneeling on my tenant Ellie's bathroom floor and had my head and shoulders under the sink, which had been draining slowly and was now clogged.

Ellie lives in the laneway house at the bottom of my backyard. She is a strong, independent woman herself, but balks at doing home repairs. She says they chip her nail polish.

"It's the one that looks like a wrench, but with long handles." I pointed toward my toolbox.

"Looks like a what?"

I was fairly certain she was playing dumb for her own amusement. I gave her a saucy look and leaned over and grabbed the tool. The nuts at either end of the p-trap weren't coming unscrewed, and I needed more leverage. I put the mouth of the channel lock over one nut and gave it a push.

"Where was I, honey? Oh, yes—Tyler's meltdown."

Ellie was sitting on the edge of the tub, her legs crossed at the knee and one manicured hand draped over said knee. She was wearing a long blue dress with white polka dots that was fitted through the bodice and then flared down to her calves. Her feet were bare and her toenails were painted gold. She never failed to look like she was about to attend a cocktail party at a diplomat's mansion. She was 'entertaining' me (her word, not mine) by recapping the plot of some ridiculous reality show. It sounded to me like all the participants were morally bankrupt narcissists, but maybe I was feeling cranky because the painting I'd been working on before Ellie knocked on my back door was not turning out the way I'd hoped.

"So then Tyler says that he only slept with Jessica because Amber had ignored him at the backup dancer group date…"

I let Ellie's words wash over me. The nut loosened and I was able to unscrew it all the way with my hand.

"And then Nathan got involved and he was all pissed off because…"

I loosened the nut at the other end of the p-trap and waited while some water spilled out into the plastic container I'd placed on the floor of the cupboard.

Ellie was still talking. "…which I think is odd because she's just not that type of girl."

I pulled the p-trap off the pipes at either end and kept my gag reflex in check when I looked inside. I had an urge to hand the pipe to Ellie and make her clean it out, but I reached two fingers inside and pulled. A long, fuzzy-but-wet glob of hair came out as I pulled. And kept pulling. I dropped it into the plastic container.

"Ew. Gross." Ellie wrinkled her nose.

"Don't 'Ew, gross' me. That's your hair, m'lady. Do you

want to clean this out?" I held the pipe up toward her and she stiffened and gripped the edge of the tub, ready to bolt.

"Do. Not. Even," she said, her flippancy about home repairs gone.

I tapped the U-shaped piece of pipe on the side of the plastic container and more hair barfed out.

"So what do you think Laura should do?"

I fished around in the pipe some more and came out with more black hairy goo attached to my fingers. "Huh? I dunno. Accept a giant ring and then break up three weeks later? Isn't that what they do on those shows?"

Ellie took a deep breath and blew it out. I wasn't looking at her, but I would have bet good money she was rolling her eyes at me. "I'm talking about my friend Laura."

"What happened? Did she get dumped on TV too?"

Big sigh. "Were you listening to me?"

"Of course. Tyler and Amber and Jennifer—"

"Jessica. And no, I'd moved on from that. Laura is my friend who works at the library."

"Okay." I nodded, having no idea who she was referring to. I needed to rinse out the piece of pipe in my hands. I shuffled on my knees over toward the tub. "Scoot over," I said to Ellie.

She slid sideways, steering very clear of me, as though I had a venomous snake in my hands.

"Freddie, I need you to listen."

"I'm listening." I turned the tap on and let the water flow through the pipe. I wasn't really listening.

"Laura works at the library. You and I bumped into her when we went to the fireworks last year. Remember? We went up to that park on Trimble and someone had a radio so we could hear the music."

I grunted what I hoped sounded like agreement, though I wasn't sure I remembered. The piece of pipe seemed to be running clean, so I shook it out and stared into it, searching for any lingering hair balls. "All clear, I think." I turned toward Ellie, smiling, proud of myself.

"Her daughter has gone missing."

"Who now? Jessica?"

Ellie made a frustrated sound. Her hand flashed out, and before I knew what had happened, she'd grabbed the p-trap from me.

"Hey!"

"I need you to listen." She held the pipe up over her head.

I sat back on my heels. "Fine. I'm listening. Someone's dog is missing."

"Her *daughter*, not her dog. Laura. My friend. Her daughter is missing."

I could see the real concern on Ellie's face now, and belatedly realized we had left reality TV land and were in actual reality land. "That's terrible, Ellie. I'm sorry. She must be frantic."

Ellie was still holding the pipe over her head. "She is. She's going out of her mind."

"How old is her daughter?"

"Thirteen."

"Oh dear." A tempestuous age. I remembered it well. I flinched as a couple of memories of fights with my mother flashed in front of me.

"Normally, yes, but Emma is not the type of kid who gets into trouble. She's a good kid, and she and Laura are really close."

I didn't know what to say. I've never been a parent, but I could imagine the kind of worry that the mother of a thirteen-year-old would be experiencing in such circumstances.

Suddenly, Ellie gave a little yelp and shook herself. The pipe had dripped some water down her arm. She handed it back to me as quickly as she'd taken it away and grabbed a towel to wipe herself with.

I took the opportunity to kneel-walk back to the vanity. I

placed the p-trap back in its position and began tightening the nut from the drainpipe.

Behind me, Ellie made a quiet noise in her throat and I heard her shift around on the bathtub's edge. If I hadn't known her for as long as I had, I would have said she was nervous.

Eventually she said, "I was hoping maybe you'd help Laura out."

I glanced over my shoulder at her. I'm sure my face was all scrunched up. "Help her?"

"You helped that guy Rory recently to find his friend."

"Yes, but…" I began tightening the nut at the other end of the p-trap. "That was just…" I didn't exactly know what words to use. "…That was just a weird set of circumstances that came together."

"But you found him."

"Christopher? Sure, but I knew him. And I knew Rory. I don't know Laura."

The nuts were tight. I turned on the water valve-thingy at the back of the vanity and then reached up and turned on the tap. The water flowed easily into the drain now. Ah, the satisfaction of a job well done. "Ta-da!" I said to Ellie. She gave two half-hearted claps with her hands.

I began to tidy up the tools I'd used and pulled the plastic container out of the cupboard. "You'll have to put all your stuff back in the right place." I gestured to the bottles, jars and packets on the floor that we'd pulled out of the vanity earlier. I looked up at Ellie. She was picking at the towel in her lap, looking troubled. "Has Laura gone to the police?" I said.

Ellie's dark brown eyes met mine. She shook her head. "She's really uncomfortable with the police. She's had some bad experiences."

I nodded. "What if I got Mack to talk to her?" James 'Mack' McCormack was a close friend of mine who also happened to be a police officer.

"She wants to talk to you."

"Me?"

"She thinks you might be able to help her."

I shook my head and stood up. "I don't see how."

"You seem to have a knack for finding people," Ellie said.

I shrugged. "That was just a fluke. Like I said, it was just a strange set of circumstances that all came together." I started to move toward the bathroom door.

Ellie stood up, still holding the towel in her arms. She followed me out to her front door. "I don't think that's true. Not everyone would have done what you did for Christopher."

What Ellie was proposing seemed ridiculous to me. I am not a police officer and have never had any ambitions in that direction. I'm an artist, a painter and a sculptor, who loves nothing more than to spend a day in the south-facing studio at the back of my house. I couldn't see what Ellie was seeing in me. The situation with Christopher had come about because I knew him and wanted him to be safe, not because I had any sort of specialty at finding people who are missing. I felt like Ellie was firing her arrow at the wrong target.

I was at her front door and was about to walk back across the lawn to my house. As I turned to look at her, standing in her bare feet on the tile floor, I realized I had never seen her face look so stricken. Ellie is normally in command of any room or situation she finds herself in. Whatever was going on with her friend Laura was clearly very serious. Why she had chosen to approach me was a question I wasn't able to answer. But it was obvious that for whatever reason, Ellie really wanted my help. I couldn't explain it, but I could empathize with the pitiful look on her face.

"Fine," I said, relenting. "I'll come and meet your friend. But just know that this is an insane proposition, and probably the only thing I'm going to do is advise her to speak to the police."

Ellie gave two more short claps, her expression lifting. "Thank you so much, honey. You're the best."

I pulled open the back door and said over my shoulder, "Also, I'm going to buy you one of those sieve things to go over your drain. I don't want to go through the experience of digging your hair out of the pipes ever again."

Chapter 2

Ellie didn't waste any time getting me over to meet with her friend Laura. The next morning at 9 AM she was opening the passenger door to her enormous SUV for me. I climbed up into the seat like I was climbing a flight of stairs to get there.

"This thing is nearly as big as your house."

Ellie climbed into the driver's seat beside me. "People stay out of my way, that's for sure."

It was a short drive, and we probably could have walked, but one of the Commandments of Ellie was that she didn't walk anywhere. And given that she was wearing sling-back heels and a blue cashmere coat, it made sense. I, on the other hand, was in my winter wardrobe of jeans, slip-on boots, a black turtleneck, and a dark green waxed jacket that zipped up the front. My dark strawberry-blonde hair was pulled into a loose ponytail at the base of my neck.

Ellie was right. People did get out of her way. She tended to take up more than one lane, and I saw a few people giving us some dirty looks and maybe some middle-finger gestures. Ellie seemed oblivious to all of this, driving as though the road was solely hers and the other cars were trespassing.

Laura lived in a three-story walk-up across from a park on East 10th between Fraser and Clark Drive. Years ago this neighborhood had been pretty sketchy, but as the yuppies moved east it had gentrified. Down the block from Laura, where Ellie squeezed her vehicle into a tiny parking spot with very impressive maneuvers, there were mid-century Craftsman houses that had been lovingly renovated and restored. Some of them were painted brightly contrasting colors, which gave the neighborhood a whimsical feel.

Ellie seemed slightly nervous. I wondered if she was afraid that I was going to withdraw my offer to talk to Laura.

I still didn't entirely understand why we were here, or, more specifically, why I was here. But I figured a short conversation, and an introduction to the idea that at the very least Laura should speak to my friend Mack, would suffice. I had brought his business card specifically for that purpose.

We reached the front door of the building and Ellie pressed a buzzer on the panel. Without hearing a voice respond, I heard the front door click open and grabbed the handle reflexively.

This building had not been lovingly restored like the houses down the block. The blue swirly carpet on the floor beneath our feet was circa 1964, and I could see plywood through some worn patches. The wall to our right was entirely covered in floor-to-ceiling mirrors with a brown, dappled effect that just added to the ugliness. The left wall was covered in a bank of mailboxes. The entire place smelled of a mixture of stale cigarette smoke mixed with bacon fat and a faint hint of cat urine.

Ellie pulled open a door in the lobby and headed up the stairs with a swish of her skirts. I followed reluctantly in her wake. By the time we got to the third-floor landing, the smell of cigarette smoke had gotten much stronger, and I was trying to hold my breath against it, which wasn't working because I was puffing from coming up the stairs. The hallway was cast in gloom by the inadequate lighting, and, in hindsight, this was representative of the situation we were walking into. Before Ellie could knock on the door at the end of the hallway, it was pulled open by a tiny woman who I assumed was Laura. Without a word Ellie folded the tiny woman into her arms and they stood hugging for several moments in silence.

Eventually, Ellie stepped back but held onto the woman's hand. "Laura, let me introduce you to Freddie Lark, my landlord and my good friend."

Laura met my eyes, nodded once subtly with her chin, and then turned and disappeared into the apartment. Ellie motioned for me to follow her.

This apartment was clearly one of the sources of the cigarette smell in the hallway. Stepping into it and closing the door behind me, I felt like I was walking into a cloud of nicotine. The smell was stifling and noxious, and I wondered how anyone could bear to live in such an atmosphere.

Straight ahead as we came in through the front door was a galley kitchen, and, at a brief glance, I could see that the limited counter space was liberally covered in dirty dishes and pots and pans. We moved to our right and the suite opened up into a large living room. When I say 'large,' however, I mean by Vancouver standards. As the city continues to grow and real estate prices skyrocket, any buildings that have gone up since about 1995 have had rooms that are so small I always joke that you have to decorate with Barbie furniture. I knew people who lived in a condo downtown where, once they'd put the queen-sized bed into the master bedroom, there was no room for anything else. There were maybe six inches on either side of the bed to squeeze around, and that was it. Furniture companies had sprung up that manufactured and sold couches that were referred to as 'condo-sized,' meaning tiny.

Despite the light coming in through the wall of north-facing windows, the room was filled with a distinct air of despondency. Understandable, given Laura's circumstances.

It appeared that she had been sleeping on the sofa. There was a blanket casually tossed over one end and a pillow on the floor beside it. Laura sank into a divot at one end of the couch that embraced her with familiarity. In front of her there was a cereal bowl that was serving as an ashtray and was nearly overflowing. Also on the coffee table were two single-sized pizza boxes, a crumpled fast-food bag, and two fast-food waxed cups with straws sticking out of them.

The rest of the room was a cacophony of furniture and shelving units. A plastic TV tray circa 1972 sat in front of one of the windows at the front of the room with five or six plant pots on it, all the residents deceased. In addition to the couch, there was one small upholstered chair, liberally stained, and an old dining room chair with a torn upholstered seat. Everything was positioned facing the large television screen that hung on the wall across from the couch. There were two laminated posters with curling edges on the wall opposite the TV, depicting wide-eyed kittens and puppies. I was encouraged to see a small bookshelf filled to bursting with books of all shapes and sizes, some of them with the plastic jacket covers and cataloging stickers that marked them as library books.

Laura was clearly not a woman of tremendous means, and yet the television was state of the art and at least five feet wide. It was something about the modern age that confused me; everyone always seemed to have money for electronics.

Laura had sunk into her seat on the couch and was lighting up another cigarette, so it was left to Ellie to be the hostess. She motioned for me to sit in the upholstered chair, but I took one look at its seat and elected to sit on the old dining room chair instead. I balanced on the edge of it and kept my purse in my lap. I was feeling weighted down with Laura's despair, and was already guiltily wondering how quickly we could leave. Ellie went around and sat beside Laura and put her hand on Laura's back.

"Laura, honey, this is Freddie that I told you about. The lady who's going to help you out."

Ellie met my eyes as she said this, and I widened mine in a way that I hoped said, 'Hey, wait a minute. That's not what we agreed to.'

She barreled ahead. "Can you tell Freddie about Emma so that she can help you?"

I could feel the rip current sucking me under.

Laura lifted her chin and looked at me for the first time since we'd come into her apartment. She was a petite woman and looked even more so sitting beside Ellie. She was wearing a stained and bedraggled gray hoodie, zipped up halfway over what looked like a Mickey Mouse T-shirt. She had on black yoga pants that were too long for her, the hems frayed and dragging. Her feet were bare. Her hair was a mousy brown color that didn't quite match her fair eyebrows. It was pulled back in a loose ponytail that was off center on the back of her head; much of the hair had been pulled out of the elastic on the right-hand side. I suspected she had slept on it. Her eyes were blue and ringed with red, and her nose was red as well. Clearly, she been crying; beside the coffee table was a wicker waste-paper basket that was nearly full of crumpled tissues.

Something like hope lit Laura's eyes now. "Do you think you can find Emma?"

I started to answer, and then Ellie answered for me. "She sure can, honey. She's great at that sort of thing."

Obviously, I needed to quell Ellie's well-intentioned but misguided description of who I was and why I was here. "I think what Ellie meant to say is that I have a friend who is in the police department, and I've brought you his business card. He's a really good guy, and..."

Laura begin shaking her head vigorously, the most energetic movement I'd seen from her since we had arrived. "Nope. No cops. No way."

I leaned forward on the chair, which turned out to have

uneven legs. It shifted, and I jerked forward dramatically. "Laura, I can see that you're tremendously distraught about Emma. It's really important that we get professionals involved in whatever's happened. The police have the resources and the knowhow to be able to help you."

Laura shook her head throughout my whole speech, slowly but methodically and with conviction. When I was finished talking, she looked at Ellie. "I said no cops."

Ellie nodded, then rubbed Laura's back some more while she looked at me with wide, imploring eyes.

Laura took a firm drag on the cigarette in her right hand, inhaling as though her life depended on it, which maybe it did.

"Tell her about Emma, honey," Ellie prompted her again. "She loves to draw, too, doesn't she? Freddie is an amazing artist."

Laura brightened ever so slightly. "She does love to draw," she said, taking another drag on her cigarette. "She drew that." She pointed to the wall at the back of the galley kitchen. On it there was an ink illustration of a unicorn with a thick chain reaching down from its halter. An interesting bit of imagery from a thirteen-year-old girl.

For something to do, I walked over and had a closer look. The technique was appropriate for someone in their teens, but also quite delicate and skillful. I turned back to Laura. "She's really good."

Laura nodded vigorously; her eyes were welling with tears again. "She really is. When she's not studying, she's always drawing. Always has her sketchbook with her. I can't get her nose out of that thing." She wiped her nose with the sleeve of her hoodie and knocked the ash from her cigarette into the bowl in front of her, and then continued. "She loves school. I don't understand it, but she really likes it." She shrugged her shoulders in a 'What are you gonna do with kids these days?'

sort of way. "She can't get enough of learning and understanding new things."

All parents should have such problems, I thought.

Despite myself, I asked a question. "When did she go missing?"

Ellie gave a small, satisfied smile I tried to ignore. Laura didn't seem to know where to begin, so Ellie prompted her.

"You saw her Tuesday morning, right? Before school?"

Laura nodded. Her cigarette was now burned down to the filter. She stubbed it out in the pile of others in the bowl and immediately lit up another one. "She went to school, just like regular, on Tuesday morning. My shift at the library didn't start until eleven, so I was here when she left. And then she had math club after school," Laura gave a slight roll of her eyes at this, "so I knew she wouldn't be home alone too long. I got home at seven that night, and she should've been here by then, but she wasn't. I didn't worry too much about it. Sometimes when she knows that I'm working the later shift, she'll go over to her friend Olivia's house. But when she wasn't home at nine, I started to wonder if something was wrong. So I called Olivia's mom, but she said that Emma hadn't been there."

Laura seemed to run out of steam after that. She lifted a ceramic coffee cup off the table in front of her and looked into its depths. Whatever was there didn't appeal to her, and she set it down again. Ellie, noticing the gesture, stood up, saying, "I'll make us some coffee," and bustled off to the kitchen.

I could hear her rattling around out there, but that didn't stop her from calling out, "So you phoned around, right, Laura?"

In front of me, Laura nodded and said, "I called everyone I knew. I couldn't call the school, of course, 'cause they were closed by then, but I called a couple of her other friends. I didn't know anyone from the math club, so I couldn't call any of them to see if she had been there. I wasn't sure what to do."

Despite myself, again, I asked, "Does Emma have a Facebook account or Instagram?"

Laura shook her head. "No, she doesn't have a phone. She's not allowed on social media."

While Ellie worked in the kitchen, Laura, in a rambling and slightly incoherent way, told us more about Emma's habits and the normal structure of her week. Like most parents, Laura was proud of her child, and she also seemed slightly baffled by her; Emma seemed to have an intelligence and curiosity that her mother was devoid of.

Emma was, by Laura's accounts, a good student who nearly always got straight A's. I took this with a grain of salt, and perhaps it showed on my face. Seeing this, Laura got off the couch with a purposeful energy and went over to a tired-looking Ikea bookshelf, where she began rummaging around through stacks of paper and file folders. Eventually she found what she'd been looking for and brought it over to me. It was a report card, and she was right. Emma had got almost entirely straight A's; she'd got a B- in Phys ed.

I smiled at Laura and handed the report card back to her. "She's obviously an amazing girl."

"She is. She really is. That's why this whole thing is just so..." Laura flapped the report card against her leg, not knowing what word to use, and the momentary lift in her mood fell away.

Ellie appeared and silently handed Laura a cup of coffee, which she took gratefully.

"Why don't you show Freddie Emma's room?" Ellie said.

Without a word Laura turned, coffee cup in one hand and report card in the other, and walked through the living room and down a short hallway to a closed door. I followed, but pinched Ellie as I passed her in retaliation for encouraging Laura to think I'd be helping find Emma. Laura opened the door and we entered a world that was entirely unlike the living room we'd been seated in. It was clear that this was Emma's domain. I realized suddenly that Laura must not be sleeping on the couch only because of Emma's disappearance. That must be where she slept all the time. This was a one-bedroom apartment, and the bedroom had been allocated to Emma.

The room smelled slightly less of cigarette smoke, something that I assumed was a deliberate strategy on Emma's part. And in contrast to the rest of the suite, it was as neat as an army cadet's bunkhouse. There was a single bed with a pastel-green bedspread. The single pillow at the head of the bed was propped up against the wall, and in front of that sat a small, bedraggled-looking teddy bear, who was obviously deeply loved. The walls of the room were painted a pale pink color, and in spots I could see a different color underneath where the roller had missed. Perhaps Emma had painted the room herself.

Around the room's walls I counted three bookshelves, mismatched but, again, neat as a pin. The books were all lined up, spines out, and I made a silent bet with myself that if I investigated, they would be grouped in some way, by subject or by author.

Under the window at the far end of the room was a scratched wooden table with an old metal kitchen chair with a red, vinyl seat pushed under it. The table served as a desk, and there were books in a neat stack on two corners of it, along with a few tchotchkes and a mug with a broken handle filled with pens and a pair of scissors. There were a few notebooks and a couple of pads of blank paper as well. This was the heart of the room.

Posters on the wall included the periodic table of elements, a map of the solar system, a slightly worn and faded poster from the Audrey Hepburn movie *My Fair Lady*, and another of Gal Gadot as Wonder Woman. Above the desk was a poster with rows of photographs of women like Marie Curie, Mary

Jackson and Michelle Obama, with inspirational quotes beneath each.

I stood, soaking it all in. Despite myself, I was getting a better sense of who Emma was. Her personality shone through even though she was absent. I turned to say something to Laura, but she was gone, and it was just Ellie standing there with beseeching eyes. I held my hand up, cutting off whatever she was about to say.

Ellie had put me in an impossible position, and underneath my concern and empathy for Laura and Emma, I was furious with her. And I was furious with myself. I was an idiot to have agreed to come and see Laura. By showing up here, I had only given her some hope that I would help. And that was impossible. I wasn't a police officer or even a social worker, nor was I in any kind of official position to be able to assist. I didn't understand why Ellie had connected the dots between what had happened a few months ago with Christopher and with Laura and Emma's situation now. They were entirely different, and conflating the two was irresponsible on Ellie's part. She was going to get a stern talking-to from me when we got back into her urban tank.

I could feel the heat rising in my face as my thoughts made me angrier. It was time to get out of here. If I stayed, I was only contributing to the falseness of the situation. I shifted my purse and moved past Ellie, who was standing in the doorway to the bedroom, giving her a furious glare as I did so. I found Laura in the living room, once again in her spot at the end of the couch in front of the bowl of cigarette butts. As I walked toward her, I reached into my back pocket and pulled out Mack's business card. I set the card down beside the ashtray/cereal bowl.

"Laura, this is my friend Mack's business card. He's a police officer and he's a good man. I know that you'd really like him under different circumstances. He's kind, though he would hate it if he heard me describing him that way." I smiled weakly, but Laura was staring determinedly at her fingers. "You need help," I continued. "There's obviously something wrong, and Emma could be in very serious danger. You need to call the police."

Out of the corner of my eye, I saw Ellie open her mouth, beginning to object, but I barreled on.

"The seriousness of the situation calls for professional help. Whatever problems you had with the police in the past . . . you'll have to let them go."

Laura's expression became hardened for the first time since we'd walked into her apartment. "I thought that's why you were here." She glanced over her shoulder at Ellie. "I thought you said that she would help," she said accusingly, and motioned toward me with her cigarette hand.

Ellie started to speak but I interrupted her. "I'm so sorry, Laura, but the truth is that Ellie spoke out of turn. I'm not a police officer. You need to get professionals involved."

Laura dropped her chin to her chest and simply shook her head gently.

There was nothing more I could do. Staying here any longer would just give Laura more hope. Using the energy of my anger at Ellie, I turned and walked across the living room floor toward the front door. I decided that if Ellie didn't follow, I could walk home. I let myself out into the dark hallway.

Chapter 3

Ellie did follow me, but we were silent as we walked back to her monster truck. I was dealing with the simmering annoyance that she'd brought me here and tried to get me involved where I didn't belong. Ellie's face was a mask of neutrality, though she had a serious case of what my mother would call chicken-ass-mouth, her lips tightly pursed.

"I told you I didn't want to get involved and that it isn't my place," I said.

She simply nodded, and I was pissed off that I had to justify myself.

"She needs to talk to the police, Ellie. It's dangerous that she hasn't done that yet."

We passed a woman walking a black and white Shih Tzu. They were wearing matching sweaters with unicorns plastered all over.

Ellie pulled out her key fob and pressed the button. Her car beeped as we approached. I heaved open my door and made the trek up into the passenger seat. As my head cleared the seat, I startled. My sister Blythe was sitting in the back.

Now, let me back up and explain. Blythe died ten years ago. Yes, I know it's weird that I see her now and then, but it's not spooky. She looks as real to me as any other person; she just has the disconcerting habit of appearing and disappearing without warning.

As I settled into my seat and wrestled with my seat belt, Blythe got right to the point. "Why did you turn that poor woman down?"

"It would have been deeply irresponsible of me to try to help her."

"I get it, honey," Ellie replied, thinking I was talking to her. "I heard you the first four times."

Blythe carried on. "There are reasons she doesn't want to go to the police."

"I understand that," I muttered under my breath.

"I don't think you do, and I think you're being mean. And I think Mom and Dad would be horrified to know you'd refused to help that poor girl."

I turned around in my seat and glared at her. Even in the afterlife she was still a bossy older sister. "Leave me alone, would you? I'm not a cop and I'm not a … a… *detective*. What if something goes wrong? What if it's dangerous?"

I turned back around and saw Ellie staring at me, her eyes wide. She turned her head and looked into the back seat and then back at me. "Everything okay, honey?"

"Yes, fine."

"It's just that you were yelling at the back seat there."

"Sorry." I shifted uncomfortably, embarrassed. "I feel like I have a demon on my shoulder." When I said the word 'demon' I turned around again and glared at Blythe. She stuck her tongue out at me.

Ellie pushed the starter. "Alright, sweetie, but you let me know if we need to go see a doctor or anything. Auntie Ellie will be happy to drive you." She flicked her eyes at me warily.

"I'm fine. Let's go."

The three of us were quiet while we pulled out onto the street. Ellie drove east and turned at the next corner. When we got to Broadway, she put on her right turn indicator and waited while the traffic flowed by.

I sat in my seat, fuming at Blythe. When she was alive, there was no one who could annoy me as quickly or as ferociously as she could. And she knew it. One of her favorite pastimes when we were kids was to wind me up into a lather and then wait until I got myself into trouble for hitting her or trying to strangle her in my rage. Clearly, she hadn't lost the skill, even though she was dead.

I hoped she would just disappear, as she always did, but when I turned my head ever so slightly to the left, I could still see her in my peripheral vision. And worse, she caught me.

"What if it was Pickle who was missing?" she said as I flicked my head forward again. "She, or he, would be almost the same age as Emma now."

I groaned.

Ellie shot me a worried glance and then turned back to watching the traffic.

Just before Blythe died, she had been making arrangements to adopt a child. She had never been married, but her biological clock had been raging for a couple of years. Finally, she realized she didn't need a man in order to be a mother. As soon as she'd made the decision to adopt, her demeanor changed. For years there had been a simmering grumpiness and dissatisfaction about her. But once the adoption process was in motion, she was back to her normal cheery, if slightly bossy, self.

She and I had named the impending child 'Pickle.' It started as a joke and then became the word we used all the time. We never said, "When the adoption goes through…" We'd said, "When Pickle is here…" All of us—our parents, me, Blythe—fell in love with that child before it was a reality. I'd never wanted children myself, but I had planned to be the best damn aunt the world had ever seen.

Blythe had mortgaged herself to the hilt and bought a tiny

two-bedroom house in Kitsilano. For months, she spent every evening and weekend painting the walls and ripping out the 1980s carpet, burning off anticipatory energy and trying not to lose her mind while she waited for the wheels of the adoption process to slowly grind.

And then she was killed when a tree fell on her car in a storm.

She knew how much I loved the hypothetical Pickle. She knew how much I longed to teach my niece or nephew how to ride a bike and how to whistle and how to sing "Ta Ra Ra Boom De Ay" on long car rides.

And she was using that knowledge against me now. Dirty pool.

Ellie pulled into a break in the traffic and headed west, back toward Main Street.

"Turn right," I said at the next cross street.

"What?" Ellie glanced at me, puzzled, and missed the turn.

"Go back."

Her face lit up. "Really?"

"Yes, really. Go back. Quick, before I change my mind."

Ellie squealed like a nine-year-old girl and sped up, nearly side-swiping a postal truck that was trying to pull into the traffic.

I turned around in my seat to glare at Blythe, but she was gone.

Chapter 4

I lay awake that night, unable to sleep. Four or five times, I convinced myself I needed to get up and cross the back lawn and let Ellie know that I wouldn't be able to help Laura out after all. But then I'd remember the way that Laura had burst into tears when we went back to her apartment and told her that I would look into where Emma could be. Her hardened demeanor had cracked momentarily. 'Thank you' was all that she had been able to choke out between sobs.

The doubts that I had about whether or not I'd be able to help swirled around in my head for hours. The trouble was, I had no idea where I would even begin. This worry swam around in my head, like a circling shark smelling blood in the water. Because of the fear it created, I couldn't see anything else. When a predator is circling you, your focus needs to be entirely on that animal. I tossed and turned in my bed, flopping around from my back to my sides to my back again.

Then, mercifully, at about 5:30 am, when the sky began to lighten nearly imperceptibly, a metaphor for the relationships in our lives popped into my head, and the shark swam away. I think the metaphor was something I had heard related to when those we love are ill or dying. In my mind's eye, I saw a group of concentric rings, like ripples on a pond. The tightest ring at the center is where the people who are closest to us sit; in Emma's case, this was her mother, Laura. And all of the rings moving outward were the other relationships in Laura's and Emma's lives. I had started at the center with Laura, and now what I needed to do was move out to the next ring level. This picture of the concentric rings gave me hope. I didn't have a plan, but I had an idea, and in the fading darkness it was enough to get me started.

The previous afternoon, when Laura had calmed down and stopped thanking me, I'd gone into Emma's room and taken a piece of paper and a pen from her desk. I'd taken them back out to the living room and asked Laura a few preliminary questions about their life.

Emma's father was long gone, Laura said. And she didn't have any contact with him or with his family. My impression was things had not ended well. Laura was stilted and twitchy when she shared this, and I could tell she wanted to move on from talking about her ex as quickly as possible. Laura wasn't close to her own parents, she said, and she didn't have any siblings. So there wasn't really much to go on in that area, but in a way this was good. The available options for where Emma could have gone were small, and hopefully that would make my job easier.

When I pressed Laura about where she thought Emma might be, she became somewhat rambly. On the one hand, she didn't think Emma was a runaway. She described their relationship as solid and open. But on the other hand, the possibility that Emma had run away seemed to be the explanation that fitted the best. Emma knew not to talk to strangers or go anywhere with them. Laura and Emma had a password that only they knew. Emma had been taught that if anyone, under any circumstances, approached her saying her mother had sent them, they had to give the password before Emma would agree to go with them.

It took some coaxing, but eventually Laura revealed that she and Emma had been arguing more than usual lately. Emma was acting out somewhat, wanting to spend more time with friends and being slightly less obedient than she'd always been. It was nothing out of the ordinary for someone her age, Laura said, but in the few days before she'd disappeared, Emma's nose had been particularly out of joint because Laura wouldn't let her go to a concert with a group of friends.

While stranger danger was top of mind for me, based on what Laura said, it sounded like the more likely scenario was that Emma was acting out and had decided to stay with a friend without telling her mother, likely to punish her for restricting her freedom.

With faint pre-dawn light creating shadows in my room, I got up and climbed into my slouchiest, comfiest bathrobe. The street lights were still on outside as I padded down the stairs to the main floor. Years ago I had converted part of the dining room into an office area for myself. It was where my computer sat and where I paid my bills and checked Facebook and stuff like that. I rummaged around on the built-in bookshelf beside the desk and eventually found what I was looking for: a small spiral notebook.

If I was going to do this, I needed to do it properly. Blythe had ensured that I was emotionally invested. There was no sense half-assing it. This job needed my whole ass.

I went from the dining room to the kitchen and found my purse. I rummaged around and dug out the two school photographs of Emma that Laura had given me. I taped one into the inside cover of the little notebook, and then, standing at the kitchen island, I transferred the notes I'd scribbled on the piece of paper at Laura's place into the notebook. On one hand I felt ridiculous, like a pretend Harriet the Spy. And on the other hand, I told myself that what I was doing made sense. Laura needed help. She clearly was entirely unwilling to go to the police, for whatever reason. I felt like there was a backstory there, but it didn't seem appropriate to get into it yesterday.

Blythe and I had been raised by a pair of quintessential hippies. Our mom and dad, Stella and Walter, had come of age during the 60s and 70s and had taken the values of peace, love, and understanding onboard 100 percent. Additionally, they were, and are, entrepreneurial at heart. When Blythe and I were children, Stella and Walter owned and ran one of Vancouver's first health food stores, on West Broadway near Alma. Somehow, despite their hippie sensibilities and moral objection to rampant capitalism, they had managed to be a huge success, and we grew up in comfortable circumstances. After Blythe died, they sold our Dunbar home for easily ten times what they had bought it for years ago. Now they had an alpaca farm in a quiet valley in British Columbia's interior.

My parents were such hippies that our last name, Lark, was actually a name that they had chosen together when they got married. I got the impression that both sets of grandparents had been slightly horrified at this development, but it didn't seem to bother Stella and Walter.

"The lark is the herald of the dawn," my dad always used to say when anybody asked about the name. He really liked the symbology of it all.

On the outside Walter looks like a disorganized mess; his hair always needs cutting, he rarely shaves, and when he does, he tends to miss several spots and always has random, uneven patches of hair on his chin or cheek. He buys all his clothes at thrift stores because, for as long as I've been alive, he has abhorred the waste and the cruel employment practices of the fashion industry. He swears a lot, far too much for my mother's taste, and Blythe and I both picked up that habit very young. People underestimate his savvy though, at their peril. His appearance is completely out of alignment with his sharp and organized mind.

Despite being a pot aficionado before it was cool, and a

tendency to want to 'stick it to the man' at any and every opportunity, Walter is a very logical and methodical person, and that is where I get my organizational tendencies. This instinctive need to find the notebook and write everything down was entirely based on what I had modeled from my father.

Stella and Walter had also raised me to be an independent thinker, and not to ask for permission when asking for forgiveness would do. I suspected that this was the part of myself that I was connecting with when it came to finally accepting the task of finding Emma.

When I finished making all my notes in the notebook and had finished my second cup of coffee, the street lights had flickered off and I could see a light on inside Ellie's home as well. It was time to get started in earnest. I headed back upstairs for a shower.

Chapter 5

According to Laura, Olivia Tan was Emma's best friend. Olivia lived two blocks away from Laura's apartment, and that's where I was headed now: the next ring on Emma's circle. I was hoping to catch the family before Olivia left for school.

The address that Laura had given me turned out to be a Vancouver special, an architectural style of house that is unique to the city and was made popular in the late 1960s. Homes in this style are wide and boxy, with a shallow roof line and, usually, a balcony across the second floor at the front. They were built for functionality, not to please the eye. The Tan house was typical of the style, with white stucco on the second floor and a brick facade on the ground floor. The lot was bordered by a low wrought iron fence with square brick posts that matched the house facade. Each post had a white ornamental ball atop it, and the posts on either side of the gate each had a white planter. As it was November, the planters were empty of everything but soggy-looking soil and a few dead leaves.

I let myself in through the gate and knocked at the Tans' front door, feeling nervous and unsure what kind of reception to expect from this family. I had asked Laura about them, but she hadn't known much, which was somewhat surprising. I would have thought the two moms might have connected, given that their daughters were close. But what did I know? I wasn't a parent.

The door was answered by a boy who looked to be about eight years old. He was dressed in jeans and a T-shirt, with bare feet and tousled hair; he held a half-eaten piece of toast in his left hand. He didn't say anything after he opened the door but just stood staring at me, chewing.

"Is your mom home?"

Without a word the boy turned and walked up the stairs on the right of the foyer I was looking at, leaving the front door wide open, and called out at the top of his lungs, "Ma!"

The entryway was small and unadorned. In addition to the staircase, there was a closet on my left and a closed door straight ahead. After a couple of minutes of standing at the open door alone, I was wondering if I should knock again or ring the doorbell. I was debating about the protocol when a woman came down the stairs looking slightly frazzled and pulling on a sleek black suit jacket over a blouse. Mrs. Tan, I presumed. She looked at me quizzically.

"Can I help you with something?"

I apologized for dropping by so early in the morning. "My name is Freddie Lark and I'm here on behalf of Laura Reid. I'm looking into the disappearance of her daughter Emma."

"Disappearance? What do you mean disappearance?" Mrs. Tan's tone was clipped and straightforward, and her facial expression matched. She tugged and straightened the jacket hem. Below it, she was wearing a black skirt that fit her tiny frame like a glove. Below that, black tights and sensible black shoes with a low heel.

"Emma didn't come home from math club on Tuesday night," I explained, "and Laura has asked me to see if I can find out where she went or where she might be."

Mrs. Tan, who until that moment had been a buzzing hive of impatience and get-the-family-out-the-door energy, was suddenly very still. "I didn't know that."

"I think she called you on Tuesday evening asking if Olivia had seen Emma?" I phrased it as a question, trying not to be accusatory.

"That's right, but then I didn't hear anything more and I assumed everything was OK."

"Ma!" came a rallying cry from above us. "I can't find my sneakers."

Mrs. Tan waved me inside. "Come in, come in. You'll have to talk to me while we're getting ready. We're already a bit late."

She took me up the flight of stairs and through to the kitchen at the back of the house. Unfamiliar scents swirled around me. In the kitchen were the boy who had answered the door, another boy who looked to be about 10 or 11 years old, and a girl Emma's age who I assumed was Olivia. The three children were sitting at a classic red Formica kitchen table from the 1950s with a tiny Asian woman who had salt-and-pepper hair and twinkling eyes. As we entered the kitchen, a stream of what I assumed was Mandarin or Cantonese came out of Mrs. Tan's mouth.

In response to the torrent of words, the girl I assumed was Olivia, who was eating a bowl of rice with something I didn't recognize on top of it, shook her head but stayed mute.

Mrs. Tan went over to the kitchen counter where there were three soft-sided lunchboxes laid open, waiting to be filled. She moved back and forth from the fridge to the counter with lightning efficiency, adding juice boxes, fruit, and other lunch items to the kits.

"Olivia, tell this lady—" She turned to me. "I'm sorry, I've forgotten your name."

"Freddie. Freddie Lark."

"Olivia, tell Miss Lark when you last saw Emma."

Olivia looked startled. Behind glasses with dark frames, her wide eyes shifted from her mother to me and then back again. She was chewing slowly, and I got the impression she was processing everything that was going on.

Another stream of foreign-to-me instructions from her mother seemed to jolt her into being able to speak.

"I saw Emma at school on Tuesday?" She phrased the statement as a question.

"Was she at math club that afternoon?" I asked her.

Olivia nodded her head and I waited for more information, but that was all I got.

"Are you in math club too?"

Another nod.

"When you and Olivia left the school grounds, did you walk home together?"

"Yes. Until we got to her street. Then I came the rest of the way myself."

This made sense. The Tans lived a little farther from the school than where Laura's apartment was.

I kept digging. "Had she talked about running away? Had she had a fight with her mom that you were aware of?"

While Olivia and I were having this conversation, the two boys were speaking between themselves, making faces at each other and laughing. They both had food liberally splattered around their mouths. Mrs. Tan and Grandma were also carrying on a conversation between them in their Asian dialect. The room was noisy and chaotic, and I was having trouble focusing. I gave silent thanks for my quiet life.

It took Olivia a moment, but she finally answered my questions, continuing to chew her breakfast thoughtfully. "She fought with her mom sometimes." She thought about this for a moment more. "Emma was complaining about some stuff lately, but still, I think they are pretty close, especially since it's just the two of them." As she said this, Olivia glanced around at her brothers, her grandmother, and her mother. She seemed like a quiet, thoughtful kid, and I wondered what it was like for her living in a house full of chaos.

I had more questions, but at that point Mrs. Tan began zipping up the lunch kits and said, "Everybody get your backpacks. Time to go."

The window I had was closing.

"Olivia, was Emma unhappy? Had she said anything about wanting to leave or about moving away?" I was grasping at straws.

Olivia's eyes flicked over to her mother and then back to me, and she shook her head. I got the impression there was something there, but she wasn't going to say it in front of her mother.

If I had thought the house was busy until that moment, I was sorely mistaken. The level of noise and activity suddenly cranked up to eleven. The three children begin dashing around the house gathering backpacks, school books, and shoes, then returned to the kitchen to get their lunches.

I reached into the crossbody handsewn bag that my mother had made me, which I had dug out of a closet that morning. It was the perfect size for lugging stuff around and I liked that I didn't have to hold onto it. The thick strap fit comfortably across me and left both hands free. I tore a page out of the notebook, found a pen at the bottom of the bag, and quickly wrote down my name, phone number, and email address. I set the paper on the counter and said to Mrs. Tan, "If you or Olivia think of anything else, please let me know."

She nodded, but I don't think she heard a word I had said. "We have to go now. I hope that you find Emma quickly."

Like being swept along in the swift current of a river, very shortly I found myself outside on the front steps. Mrs. Tan closed the door behind us and herded the children toward the sidewalk. I went over to my car and got in. Mrs. Tan got into a small green sedan and drove off. Olivia headed in one direction; the two boys went in another. I waited a few minutes, making sure that Mrs. Tan was gone, and then I climbed back out of my car.

OLIVIA WAS WALKING ALONG SLOWLY with her head bent, and I realized as I got closer that she was reading a book as she walked. A girl after my own heart. She startled slightly as I pulled up beside her, huffing from my jog down the block. I really needed to get into better shape. Standing in front of a painting easel all day doesn't exactly give a person exemplary cardiovascular health.

"What are you reading?"

Olivia tilted the book cover toward me so I could see. It was *Pride and Prejudice*.

"A classic," I said. "I was never entirely sure that Elizabeth Bennet made the right choice, despite the romantic ending of that book."

"Who would you have had her end up with?" Olivia's glasses flashed briefly as she studied me.

"Maybe no one. She's smart and capable."

"She didn't have much of a choice, though, in her day, did she?"

"You're right."

Olivia brought me back to the present moment. "You want to ask me more questions about Emma." She phrased it as a statement. This quiet girl was no dummy.

"I felt like there was something you didn't want to say in front of your mom back there."

I thought I detected a slight dip in her chin, acquiescence about what I'd said, but she was silent. I let the silence stretch, although it was uncomfortable for me. Tension tends to make me chatty.

We came to a cross street, and up ahead I could see the school and its surrounding playground on the next block. I had a limited amount of time before I would lose Olivia again.

We crossed the street and turned right, walking parallel to the chain-link fence that bordered the schoolyard. Ahead of us I could see the break in the fence, the gate where a steady trickle of young people was entering.

Finally Olivia spoke up. "You're very observant."

"Thank you."

"It's not a compliment." Olivia had inherited some of her mother's frankness, it seemed. "My ma says we shouldn't observe life, we should live it." She glanced down at her feet as she said this, and I could see this was a message she was used to hearing.

"I like to observe things because it helps me to appreciate them," I said.

Olivia glanced up at me, skeptical. We continued walking. A girl in black jeans with a colorful poncho-cape thing slung over her shoulders called to Olivia from near the schoolyard gate and waved. Olivia waved back and then turned toward me and stopped walking.

"Is this what you do for a living? Look for missing people?"

"No. I'm just doing this for Emma's mom. My real job is as an artist."

Olivia screwed up her face slightly. "What kind?"

"I paint pictures. And I also do a little sculpture."

"And you make money doing that?"

"Some."

I could see her thinking about this. When she spoke again, her comment surprised me. "Jane Austen was an observer," she said, her face serious.

"That's right," I said. "She was a keen observer of human interaction and the social conventions of her time."

Olivia glanced down at the book in her hand and then

back up at me. There was a hesitant pause and then she said, "There's a boy Emma likes."

I caught my breath but tried to play it cool. "What's the boy's name?"

"Justin Poole." I detected a note of distain in her voice.

"You don't think too much of Justin."

"He's not very nice to Emma. He's kind of mean. But she says that he is nicer when they're alone doing homework." She turned and began walking again.

I kept in step with her. "Does Justin go to this school?"

We had reached the gate in the fence. Olivia turned, her battered copy of *Pride and Prejudice* pressed against her chest. "He's a grade ahead of us."

The distinctive shrill ring of the school bell shattered the peaceful morning, and the activity of the schoolyard became more purposeful as the children funneled themselves toward a double door under a square awning.

"I gotta go," Olivia said.

"Thanks for your help. I really appreciate it."

Olivia started to walk through the gate and then turned back. "Are you going to find her? I really miss her. I'm worried."

I didn't know what to say. Was I going to be able to find Emma? "I'll do my best," I finally said.

Olivia nodded and turned away. I wasn't sure she believed me.

Chapter 6

I had about three hours to kill before the school broke for lunch. My plan was to go back and try to find the infamous Justin. Meanwhile, I thought I would use the morning to try to find out more about Emma's presence online to see if that would be of any assistance. Laura had said that Emma didn't have a phone and wasn't allowed to have social media accounts. I had wondered if it had to do with concern about the cost of not only the phone but the monthly data plan. Laura worked as a library assistant in the Vancouver Public Library system. It was a good job, according to Ellie, for someone who didn't have more than a high school education. But I doubted that the pay would extend to phones and data plans for her 13-year-old. Even so, kids had a way of keeping things from their parents, and I wanted to do some checking myself.

The closest library branch was several blocks west, where Main Street and Kingsway converge. It was a balmy November morning and it wasn't raining, which was both welcome and unusual, so I decided to walk over to the library branch and use their computers rather than using my phone. I hadn't had breakfast yet, so I found a café and got a muffin and a coffee and ate them at the counter by the window, watching the buses trundle down Main, packed to the gills with commuters and students. I didn't regret for one second leaving that world behind.

Twenty minutes later, my belly full of sugar and caffeine, I went across the street to the library to begin my search for Emma.

I searched all the usual places: Facebook, Instagram, Twitter. There was a new social media platform that I had heard people referring to called Snapchat and another called Tik Tok. I had no idea what either of these were, so I did a little digging. Tik Tok was apparently very popular with young people and involved sharing very short videos via the app.

For more than an hour I dug around, trying to find any trace of Emma. I was by no means experienced with trying to find people online, but I did all the usual things, which mostly involved searching for her name via Google. I saw that Olivia had an Instagram account, but it was private. I decided to widen my search and began looking for any accounts that Laura might have online, but came up empty there as well, which was unusual. I found Olivia's mom, Hyacinth Tan, on Facebook, although her account privacy settings were airtight, meaning I couldn't see her friends. It was a frustrating and fruitless way to spend a couple of hours. I was staring out into space, wondering what else I could look for, when a young woman tapped me on the shoulder.

"Are you done there?"

I got to my feet and gathered my things. It was time for me to give up my seat and let someone else have a turn.

As I walked back to my car, feeling baffled and not a little frustrated, I realized I hadn't noticed a phone in Laura's apartment suite, and there definitely wasn't a computer. Although there could have been a cell phone tucked away in her purse or some other place I couldn't see it. I hadn't thought to check Canada411 for whether or not she had a landline. Regardless, it seemed inconceivable that, in the twenty-first century, a person could not have any kind of presence online, but I supposed it was possible.

As I climbed into the driver's seat and stowed my stuff on the passenger seat beside me, I wondered about how to go about finding this Justin individual. It turned out to be much easier than I expected.

~

AT 12:05 the school bell rang again, and shortly thereafter teens and tweens begin spilling out of every visible doorway. My plan was to simply start asking around, to go up to a couple of random kids and ask where Justin Poole was and see where that led me. I was staring through the windscreen, working up my nerve, when there was a rap on the glass beside my left ear. I jumped and turned in my seat and found the faces of three teenage boys staring at me through the window, laughing. I rolled down the window with the crank handle.

"Can I help you?"

The boy in the center of the trio said, "Hey, pedo. Whatcha doin' hanging around outside a school?"

He looked to be about five foot six and he was all knees, elbows, and chin. From what I could see, he had dark brown hair, most of it hidden under a baseball cap with a very flat brim and a symbol on the crown that I didn't recognize. He was wearing an oversized leather jacket and jeans that looked like they were about to fall off him. His two chums were dressed similarly, and all three had looks on their faces of snide superiority mingled with uncertainty.

Astonishingly, I felt slightly intimidated. I decided that wouldn't do. I opened the car door and got out, closing it behind me. Now I was taller than all three of them. Amazing what a strength height is.

I shoved my hands in my jeans pockets. "Who are you?"

"Who am I? Who are *you*? I heard you was looking for me."

Ah, so this was the famous Justin.

"I understand you know Emma Reid," I said.

"What about her?" he answered, and the two boys beside him smiled at how clever he was. They were obviously easily amused.

"You know she's missing, right?"

"What's that to me?" Justin turned and sniggered at his two friends.

"Are you Emma's boyfriend?"

"That brainer? No way." The three boys laughed again and pushed one another's shoulders, jostling about; they reminded me of a small litter of puppies.

These were boys in a liminal place; not quite grown men, but not children either. And they were working really hard to leave childhood behind, as perhaps we all do at that age. Behind the street cred, gangsta clothes, and attitude I could see the little boys they had recently been. A year earlier, they had probably been playing army men or cowboys in their yards. It made me sad.

"What do you mean 'brainer'?" I asked Justin.

"I mean brainer, man. Don't you know what that means?"

"Enlighten me."

He looked confused for a second. "She's all smart and stuff, yo. She gets good grades and she sucks up to all the teachers." Justin turned and said something to his friends that I didn't catch. The other two boys laughed like they were watching Jerry Seinfeld at the Apollo.

"So she's interested in getting an education, and you think that's a bad idea."

The wattage of Justin's smile dimmed, but then he recovered. "Who needs an education, man, when this is a free market economy? Hustle is how you get ahead." He sounded like he was quoting someone. A parent, perhaps?

"Why would people think that Emma is your girlfriend?"

"I don't know, man. Who knows what bitches say when they're talking? Maybe it was wishful thinking."

"Aspirational?"

Justin's eyebrows came together slightly. "I guess, man. Whatever that means." The three boys jostled one another again, though some of the mirth had gone out of their performance.

"But you know Emma, right?"

"Sure. I see her around."

"But you're not friends with her."

"She lets me copy her homework, that's all."

Now the situation was becoming clearer. Mr. Free Market Economy was using Emma's brain to get ahead in the education he didn't believe in.

"When you were copying her homework, did she ever say that she was planning on running away?"

Some of Justin's bravado returned. "Nah. I don't listen to what she has to say. I just need the digits off her math homework, yo."

I crossed my arms over my chest. I was having to physically prevent myself from reaching over and strangling Justin until his eyes popped out of his smarmy little head. He was being brutally honest, likely to impress his two sidekicks. But I sensed something else underneath the bravado. There was a tension around his eyes that the joshing around and being cool wasn't hiding.

"Are you sure you don't know anything about Emma being missing?" I said.

The energy of the three boys dimmed again. They glanced awkwardly at one another and avoided meeting my eyes. Finally, Justin said, "Maybe she's gone to nerd college."

His two sidekicks guffawed at this hilarity.

"Do you have any idea where she'd go?"

"How should I know?" Justin shook his head. "I'm not the nerd police." His posture changed and he took a step back from where he'd been standing. "Yo, is that it, lady? We gotta go. Got no time for hanging around with pedophiles like you."

"It's a shame about Emma," I said. "Now who's going to do your homework for you?"

Justin and the other two boys laughed. "Oh, don't you worry, lady. There's always another brainer who will let me crib off her."

The three boys started to walk away, laughing and crowing about how clever they were.

It was a good thing Justin's mother, wherever she was, couldn't hear the names I was calling him in my head.

———————————————

Chapter 7

———————————————

Sitting in a car all afternoon is not my favorite way to spend my time. After Justin and his sidekicks left me, I went back over the conversation in my head. I revisited the feeling that, beneath the attitude and bravado, it felt like he was hiding something. It might have absolutely nothing to do with Emma's disappearance, but I had to know. It was about the only thread I had to pick at.

I took myself over to Main Street for lunch at a hipster café and had a greasy quesadilla and a cup of coffee that wasn't nearly as hot as it should've been. Then back to the library for another hour of searching online for any sign of either Emma or Laura. It had started to rain while I was eating and continued off and on throughout the early part of the afternoon. By the time I gathered my notes and began to walk back toward the school, I was glad I had thought to bring my umbrella with me.

My car, a 1989 dark blue VW Jetta named, naturally, Loretta, was where I'd left her. She wasn't sexy or even very attractive, but she made up for that by being reliable. Mostly.

My friends teased me about Loretta, saying I should trade up for something newer and more likely to start at the first turn of the key. But we were a bonded pair who had been through a lot together. I also objected to how throw-away our culture had become. I would stick with Loretta until she decided it was her time to go to the big scrap heap in the sky.

I moved her to a spot where I could see several of the doors leading out of the junior high school. It was entirely possible that I would miss seeing Justin. That he would have a basketball practice after school or that he would leave by an exit on the other side of the building. It wasn't possible for me to watch all the entrances at once, but I decided to give it a shot. In the concentric rings of Emma's life, Justin, despite his protestations, seemed like a ripple who was closer to Emma than he wanted to let on.

Luck was with me. Through Loretta Jetta's rain-splattered windscreen I caught sight of Justin and his two buddies about five minutes after I heard the bell ring, signaling the end of the school day. They walked through the schoolyard, playfully shoving and teasing one another. It was clear from the boys' body language that Justin was the ringleader. He was slightly more aloof than the other two. When they got out onto the sidewalk, one of them gave the other two a complicated series of hand bumps and then peeled off, walking east on the side street. Justin and the remaining boy crossed the street and headed south, toward Broadway.

I had never followed anybody in my life, let alone a 14-year-old boy, and right now I had absolutely no idea what I was doing. But I figured I had nothing to lose, and I would just do my best and see how it turned out.

When the boys had disappeared from my view, I cranked Loretta's engine, and she cooperated on the third try. I crept along to the side street where the boys had disappeared. I saw them up ahead, continuing to walk toward Broadway. There was a pedestrian-controlled light, and I saw them push the button and wait. When the light changed and allowed them to cross the street, I pulled forward and then, as I got close to

Broadway, pulled into an illegal parking space too close to the corner.

The boys walked east, and I realized that if they continued to walk, I might have to get out of the car. I wasn't sure how that would go, and it seemed there would be a greater likelihood they would spot me. Thankfully they positioned themselves at a bus stop, standing outside the shelter, too cool to be bothered by the rain.

I waited, and in a few short minutes a number nine trolley bus squealed to a halt at the stop. I was leaning forward, gripping the steering wheel more tightly than necessary. I tried to remember what bus routes would be running along Broadway and figured that the number nine was the only one at this part of the route. So it was likely that this was the bus the boys had been waiting for. The bus pulled away from the curb, and sure enough, the boys were gone. I leapt out of the car, ran to the pedestrian control, pushed the button, and then ran back to the car, climbed in, and waited. The light turned and I pulled out onto Broadway and followed the bus.

Buses, it turns out, are easy to follow. What was a little more difficult was keeping watch at each stop to see whether or not Justin got out. I kept well back, keeping several car lengths between Loretta and the back of the bus, hoping the boys weren't staring out the back window. The bus had looked full, crammed with student commuter traffic, when I was sitting on the side street, so I hoped that the boys were jammed in at the front somewhere. At each stop, when the bus pulled away, I would peer through the windscreen, looking for Justin. We traveled all the way along Broadway to Commercial Drive like this—the bus stopping every block and a half or so and me peering out over Loretta's steering wheel like Mr. Magoo. Every once in a while, a car behind me would get frustrated, pull out into the center lane, and zoom past.

Eventually the bus turned left at Commercial Drive, where there is a Sky Train station. My heart sank. If Justin got off the bus here and got onto the Sky Train, there was very little chance that I could park the car, buy a ticket, and follow him onto whichever train he was catching. There were three different lines that intersected at that station, and I'd lose him for sure.

I held my breath and watched as the bus pulled away from the Sky Train stop. It had disgorged dozens and dozens of passengers. I pulled ahead and scanned the crowd, looking for Justin. Up ahead, the bus went through a traffic light, which turned yellow and then red. I lingered, continuing to scan the crowd, figuring that I wouldn't lose the bus. I didn't see him, but I couldn't be sure that I had missed him either. I decided to pull ahead, and when the light turned green, I caught up to the bus, scanning the sidewalk in case it had let Justin out at the bus stop after the Sky Train station. It was exhausting work, and my neck and back were tight from straining forward, trying to see.

I figured that the bus would terminate before it got to East Hastings Street. I didn't use public transit that often, preferring to walk everywhere I could, and I wasn't sure where that happened. I could see that space had opened up inside it; it was no longer a can of sardines.

I drove along slowly, chewing one of my thumbnails, and thinking we had to be near the end of the line. Perhaps I had missed him, I thought glumly. I tried to reassure myself that tomorrow was another day and I could always go back to the school again and pick up the search. That was one thing about kids; you always knew where they would be between nine and three-thirty.

But suddenly, my persistence was rewarded. The bus crept over a tiny rise and then headed downhill, stopping in front of a well-known Cuban restaurant. And who should be walking along the sidewalk as the bus pulled away but Mr. Free Market Economy.

I froze, astounded that my ridiculous plan had worked. I

stayed in the curb lane, once again annoying the traffic behind me, and watched Justin as he waited at the corner. There wasn't a pedestrian-controlled light here, so he waited for a gap in the traffic and then crossed at a trot, his droopy jeans miraculously staying attached to his hips. I watched him go, still idling by the curb. When I was about to lose sight of him, I did a quick shoulder check, waited for a break in the traffic, and then scooted across the two lanes and turned left onto the side street where Justin had gone. Up ahead, I could see him turning another corner, so I crept along the side street, keeping a good bit of distance between us and praying that he wouldn't see me. When I thought it was safe once again, I turned the corner—and he was completely gone.

I drove ahead, scanning left and right, swearing under my breath. We were in a light industrial area with one-story buildings that looked like small warehouses interspersed with two- and three-story apartment buildings.

My swearing got louder now; I was furious that I had lost Justin after all that hard work. Then, as I passed one of the small warehouse buildings, I glanced left and just happened to catch a glimpse of Justin's backpack disappearing at the back of one of them. I cheered quietly to myself and begin looking for a parking space.

The front of the building that Justin had disappeared into had a sign outside that said U Bottle It. It was a winemaking facility and appeared to be open. There were two cars in the parking area at the front of the building, so I pulled in beside them. The building was plain, with just a metal door on the right-hand side and a barred window about the size of the average living room window on the left. The blinds in the window were closed. I pulled the door to the shop open and found myself in a lobby area that was the width of the building, perhaps 30 feet across. There was a high counter opposite me and signs on the walls announcing package deals on winemaking and bottling. The floor was dark linoleum, and the walls were painted a rust color, which made the reception area dark.

When I entered, there was nobody there, but very shortly a woman popped out from a door behind the desk. "Can I help you?"

Obviously, I couldn't tell her what I was actually doing. "I was wondering if you had a price list."

"Sure thing," she said.

We faced each other across the counter and she handed me a trifold pamphlet and a single sheet of paper. Pointing to the pamphlet, she started explaining to me how the wine-making process worked and what the pricing meant. I wasn't really listening. I tried to act as though I was, but really, I was trying to see through the doorway that she had come through. All I could see was a hallway and possibly a door leading off it. The place was entirely quiet. I couldn't hear other voices or movement in the building.

When she finished talking, just to keep the conversation going and to see if I could learn anything, I said, "Pretty quiet in here this afternoon."

She smiled, but there was a slight wariness in her eyes. Maybe she had clocked the fact that I wasn't really listening to her. "Weekdays are always pretty quiet," she said. "We're much busier on the weekends."

"I'm sure." I tried to think of something else to say and came up empty. I couldn't exactly ask if she knew Justin. She didn't look old enough to be his mother, and she looked a little too old to be a sister, if this was a family business.

Eventually I just thanked her for the information she'd given me and went back outside.

Justin had seemed to be going around to the back of the building, so I decided that was what my next move should be. I shoved the papers into my purse and walked down the alley that he'd taken. It ran the length of the building, and I passed a silver, two-door convertible BMW parked illegally beside a dumpster. The alley intersected with another at the back, making a T formation, and when I cautiously turned the corner, I found another door like the one I'd gone through at the front, made of metal with a very sturdy plate over the locks. Here, too, there was a window beside the door that was barred and shuttered. The door had settled into the frame, but wasn't completely closed. I pulled on it, and, much to my surprise, it actually opened.

Chapter 8

Right away I was hit with the unmistakable smell of marijuana. I was in a small entryway; yellowed linoleum on the floor, bare fluorescent bulbs overhead, beige walls that looked like they could use a really good scrubbing, and two doors, one straight ahead and one on my right. That was it. No furniture. No decoration. Just floor, walls, ceiling, and doors. I stood still for a second, listening. The first thing I noticed was a low humming noise, but beyond that there wasn't any sound.

My heart was thumping in my chest and I was feeling slightly dizzy, but whether or not that was from the smell or from anxiety, I wasn't sure. I wiped the palms of my hands on my jeans and walked over to the door that was straight ahead and grabbed the handle. I pulled. But it was locked.

"Let's see what's behind door number two," I muttered to myself. I turned and walked over to the other door and this one opened.

Behind the door was a room about as wide as but much longer than a double-car garage. The low hum that I'd noticed was coming from this space. There were several fans positioned around the room: hanging from the ceiling in the furthest corners, and positioned on tables or pedestals at other spots. The room was entirely filled with tables, laid out in long rows, and each table was filled with pots of marijuana plants. There were also larger plants down the right-hand wall of the room. These were as tall as me, in huge planters like you'd use outside your home, maybe on your front walk. Hanging from the ceiling above the tables were dozens of lights, obviously there to encourage growth.

There were three people in the room, and they were just as startled by my entrance as I was by what I'd stumbled into. Justin was the first person I noticed. He was standing near the middle of the room with what looked like a pair of gardening clippers in his hand. Further back, almost touching the back wall, was another young man. At a quick glance, I figured he was probably three or four years older than Justin and looked similar to him. And then, finally, there was an angry man walking swiftly toward me. He was enormous. Probably a little over six feet tall, wearing a T-shirt and jeans. His biceps needed their own postal code.

"What in the hell?" he said, surging toward me. "Who are you?"

"I'm here to talk to Justin," I said.

The man's momentum faltered for a second, and he turned and looked at the boy, who now, unlike at our encounter earlier, really did look his age. The bravado and cockiness that had been there near the school was entirely absent. His eyes flicked from Muscleman to me and then back again.

"I don't know who she is," he said, in a voice that was slightly whiny and altogether very different from the gangster tone he had put on with me earlier in the day. "She was at the school today."

Muscleman had reached me now. He took hold of one of my elbows, turned me around, and started to push me back toward the door I'd come through.

"Hey!" I said, jerking my arm out of his paw. "Don't touch me."

In the wild, one of the strategies that animals use to defend themselves is to puff themselves up and make themselves as big as possible. I tried to do this now, even though Muscleman topped me by a good six inches. Regardless, I adopted an attitude of authority, praying that it would buy me a couple of minutes.

Pot had been legalized in Canada in 2018, and individuals were now allowed to grow four plants for personal use. Clearly that law didn't apply here. This was a commercial operation, and I wasn't entirely sure of the legality of it. Pot shops had been popping up all over Vancouver since the legalization, but there seemed to be confusion, even among the legislators, about regulating the industry. The shops required licenses, and there had been a kerfuffle in the news a while back about many of the shops being shut down over licensing issues. I honestly hadn't paid very much attention because red wine and naps are my drugs of choice. Marijuana had never appealed to me, though I had no objection to its use. In fact, I had a personal belief that it was probably healthier than hard alcohol if you wanted to get a buzz on.

My authoritative attitude worked momentarily. The man looked startled; perhaps no one ever stood up to him, given his intimidating stature. I leapt in immediately, hoping to keep him on his back foot. "I'm looking for information about Emma Reid. That's why I was talking to Justin this afternoon at school."

The man looked confused. His head swiveled to Justin and then back to me. "Who?"

"A classmate of Justin's," I said. "She's gone missing."

Now the man regained some of his composure. "Well, she ain't here, lady. So bugger off." He went to reach for my elbow again, but I took a quick side step away.

"Justin, I'm pretty sure you weren't telling me the truth

earlier when you said that the only contact you had with Emma was when you borrowed her homework." As I said that last bit, Justin's face fell.

Muscleman beside me turned his head to Justin once more. "What? Have you been cheating?"

Crap. Now I'd dropped Justin in the soup. The boy looked terrified. I was starting to put it together that maybe this was his father, and perhaps that was his brother at the back of the room, who hadn't moved or said a word since I'd entered.

I tried to distract Muscleman. "A friend of Emma's mentioned that Justin might be her boyfriend. That's why I was asking him questions."

Muscleman was still staring at Justin the way a bull stares at a matador. I suspected that Justin might be in for a goring later, and I felt terrible about it. But I tried to stay focused.

Muscleman turned his head slowly back to me. "Lady, I don't know who you are or why you're here, but I've never heard of this Emma person. It's time for you to go."

He reached for my elbow again, and once more I tried to jerk it away, but this time he was ready for me. His fingers gripped my upper arm painfully and he began to push me towards the door. I tried to appeal to his parental inclinations.

"Sir, Emma is a thirteen-year-old girl, and she's gone missing. Her mother is worried sick about her."

Muscleman continued pushing me, and I tried again to appeal to the heart that might be caged inside his massive chest. "Imagine if one of your kids went missing. Wouldn't you do whatever you could to find them?"

He was unmoved. I tried resisting his momentum and failed, my boots sliding on the linoleum floor.

Then behind me, I heard a voice. "Bob, let her go. Let's hear what she has to say."

Muscleman, aka Bob, stopped pushing. I turned, and there was a woman standing next to the door I'd come through. Behind her, the door was still swinging shut, and through the gap, I glimpsed another woman. I got just a quick impression of platinum blonde hair, high-heeled boots clicking on the linoleum, and a leather jacket, possibly with a fur collar.

The door closed now, and I focused my attention again on the woman who'd spoken. She was about five foot five, built solidly, but not fat at all. Solid like a pit bull. She had long, dark brown hair that fell well past her shoulders, and thick, dark eyebrows. She had too much makeup on overtop of what looked like a rather pretty face. There were dark rings under her eyes and cigarette lines around her mouth. She looked about my age, but I suspected she was in in actuality close to ten years younger, probably in her early thirties. She had a plaid shirt on and jeans tucked into motorcycle boots.

Given the way Muscleman reacted to her presence, by immediately dropping my arm and standing quietly beside me, my guess was that this was the boss of the operation. I hoped I could work with her maternal instincts. If she had any. Looking at her cold expression, however, I didn't think my odds were great.

"Who is it you're looking for?" the woman said.

"Emma Reid. She goes to Justin's school."

"Never heard of her." The woman gave a tiny shake of her head and then looked past me toward her son, who was still standing frozen in the middle of the room in almost exactly the same position as when I'd arrived. "Do you know this girl, Jus?"

"Yeah, but we're not, like, friends or anything."

"Right," she said with finality. "You," she pointed a finger at Justin, "and you," she pointed at me, "come with me."

Chapter 9

The woman led Justin and me back out into the lobby that I'd come through and then through the door that had been locked when I'd tried it earlier. As soon as we walked through that door, I could tell we were at the back of the wine bottling business. Ahead of us was a long room with several racks of empty wine bottles and pieces of equipment I didn't recognize. The woman led us to our right and into a small room dominated by a table that ran from one side to the other. As the three of us walked into the room, she closed the door behind us. The table had several chairs around it, and she pointed at Justin and then to a chair. To me she said, "Have a seat." It wasn't an invitation. More of a command.

She sat at the head of the table, which made me smile internally. She was the CEO taking charge of this meeting. She sat in a relaxed position with her hands on the arms of her chair, but I got the sense that she was like a tightly coiled spring and could explode at any moment. I was taller than her by several inches, but she was packed with muscle and I doubted I would last more than ten seconds if we came to blows.

She gave Justin a hard stare, communicating something to

him. He held her gaze and then dropped it into his lap. Then she looked at me. "Why don't you tell me what all this is about?"

I started by introducing myself and then I explained as briefly as I could why I was there—Emma's disappearance, and the information I had that Justin and Emma were friends.

She listened attentively, fully present and crackling with suppressed energy. When I finished, I settled in my chair and waited to see what would happen.

There was a short pause while she seemed to be processing what I had said. Then she looked at Justin. "Do you know where Emma is?"

Justin shook at his head, glancing at her only briefly.

I was pretty sure he wouldn't lie to this woman. It was abundantly clear that she was the boss of this household. At this point, I was assuming that the four people I'd encountered in the grow-op room were family. Hard-ass Mom, Muscleman Dad, Justin and his brother. I also made an assumption that the family owned the legitimate wine bottling business at the front of the building as well as the possibly illegitimate pot-growing business at the back.

The woman, who still hadn't introduced herself, looked at me and gave a small shrug of her shoulders. "There you have it. Justin says he doesn't know where she is. So you can go ahead and get the hell out of my building."

I figured my best approach was to make her feel like the alpha dog, so I said, "I wondered if I'd have your permission to ask Justin a few more questions?"

She thought about this for a moment and then nodded her agreement without saying anything.

I looked over at Justin, who was still staring into his lap. "Justin, is there anything more you can tell me about Emma? Does she have any other close friends at the school besides Olivia? Anyone who she might be hiding out with?"

Justin shook his head without looking up at me.

His mom snapped at him. "Use your words!"

The boy's eyes flicked over to her and then to me. "I don't think so. She and Olivia hung out all the time. I never saw her hanging out with anyone else."

"Did she talk to you about being upset or wanting to leave home or anything?"

Justin shook his head again and then quickly followed that with words before his mom could admonish him a second time. "No. She always seems pretty happy. She likes school." He snorted with what seemed like incredulity.

I couldn't think of any other questions to ask him without repeating myself. The room was quiet, and I could hear the distant tinkling of glass bottles bumping into one another. Finally I said, "Have you seen her or heard from her since Tuesday?"

"No. I texted her yesterday but I haven't heard anything back. She always replied pretty quickly."

I was trying to think of a follow-up question about Emma's teachers when what Justin had just said set off an alarm in my head. "Emma has a phone?"

Justin looked up and held my eyes. He seemed to realize this information was both valuable and new to me.

"Yeah," he said, lifting his chin almost imperceptibly. A tiny sliver of his cocky personality from the schoolyard returned.

"Where did she get it?"

He sat up a little straighter in his chair. "I think she got it from a friend. I think she said she, like, saved up her allowance and babysitting money and stuff and bought it used from someone at school."

"Have you tried texting her in the last day or so?"

Justin nodded.

"But she hasn't answered."

He shook his head.

The woman at the end of the table, who I'd nearly

forgotten about in light of this new information, suddenly banged her flat palm on the table. "Use your words, goddammit!"

Justin and I both jumped slightly in our chairs. No wonder this kid was a bully and a cheat, if this was how he was being raised.

He looked at me. "No," he said. "She hasn't texted back since Tuesday afternoon."

I pulled out my own phone and asked Justin if I could have the number of Emma's phone. He gave it to me. I asked for the name of the friend who had sold Emma the phone, but he didn't know who it was. He seemed pretty vague on where the phone had come from.

Justin's mom leaned forward in her chair and folded her hands together on the table. She stared at me with cold brown eyes. "Are we done here?"

I stood, pushing my chair back. "Yes. Thank you so much for your time, and for Justin's time. I appreciate it. And I'm sure Emma's mother would thank you."

Justin's mom stood up as well, not acknowledging what I'd said. She opened the door to the little conference room and jerked her head at Justin. He scuttled out of the room, back to his part-time job, which I assumed was harvesting buds.

"I'll walk you out through the front," she said.

I followed her through the rooms that made up the wine bottling business, and we emerged into the lobby that I'd entered when I first arrived. The girl who had spoken to me was there behind the desk. She glanced up, and when she saw me, she looked puzzled, but Justin's mom swept me through the lobby and out into the front parking lot. Once outside, I turned to thank her for her help, but she was already gone, the metal door closing behind her.

Chapter 10

The first thing I did when I got in my front door was pour myself a large glass of red wine. The second thing I did was bring my laptop from the desk nook in the dining room to the comfy chair I had at the back of the kitchen.

My house is a mid-century Craftsman-style design that's very common in Vancouver. I bought it specifically because of the large kitchen at the back of the house that looks out onto the backyard and faces south. The back door leads on to a small porch, which I keep meaning to have enlarged into a better deck. On the inside of the kitchen there's a little extension that's the same width as the porch. It has wide windows across the back and then narrow ones on the two short walls. When I first saw the house, shortly after my sister's death and my subsequent divorce, it was in need of quite a few repairs and renovations. The bathroom upstairs and the powder room on the main floor needed to be gutted. The floors need to be refinished, if not replaced. The house needed a new roof. The entire interior needed to be repainted. It was definitely a project house, which I was not in the mood for.

However, the thing that sold me on it, from the moment I walked into the kitchen, was this little nook that I've just described at the very back of the room. On summer days the whole kitchen is flooded with light, including that nook, which is delightful. But it was on wintery, gray November days like the one we were having today that the kitchen nook was my favorite place in the house. Other homeowners might have put a table and chairs or a banquette into the spot. It would be a perfect breakfast nook. But I knew immediately upon seeing it that I would have a huge upholstered chair with a matching ottoman so that I could sit, just like I was doing right now, and either read or draw in my sketchbook.

Today the nook had become a research area, and I spent about an hour online learning about the cannabis laws in Canada, which had changed very recently. It seemed that the operation at the back of the wine bottling business lived in a gray area between legality and illegality. That mattered to me only because of Emma. Her connection to the operation through Justin, though tenuous, still gave me food for thought.

When my glass of wine was finished and my stomach was growling, I got up and started preparing supper, such as it was. I turned on my Bluetooth speaker and pulled up a playlist full of instrumental piano and cello music, which always soothed my soul, and I listened to that while I chopped vegetables and prepared some rice in the cooker.

About twenty minutes in, Ellie's face appeared at the back door. I went over and unlocked it for her. Today she was wearing a mid-calf-length brown leopard-pattern skirt and a black sleeveless V-neck top. Where I was always freezing, Ellie seemed to run hot. I don't know that I'd ever seen her inside with her toned arms covered.

She closed the door behind her, and with well-practiced steps, went to the cupboard and got herself a wine glass. "How did it go today? Did you learn anything more about where Emma could be?"

As she came over to the island, I pushed the bottle of wine toward her. "I know a little bit more than I did yesterday."

I filled Ellie in on the progress that I'd made that day, which to me felt like I'd gone one step forward and one step back. I knew a little bit more about Emma's life, but it hadn't shone any kind of light onto where she might be.

Ellie listened with her whole body, perched on one of the barstools at my kitchen island. When I finished speaking, she reached over and grabbed a carrot stick and started munching.

"You said that Olivia's house was a Vancouver Special, right?"

I nodded

"I wonder if it's possible that Olivia is hiding Emma on the ground-floor suite?"

I looked at Ellie, puzzled. "Why would you think that?"

"When you went in the front door of the house, you were probably in a little foyer. And then you went up a staircase to the second floor, right?"

I nodded again.

"One of the reasons those houses were so popular in the fifties is that they can be set up so that they're almost two independent homes. The owners often made the ground floor into a mother-in-law suite. Or they would rent it out. You can have a little kitchen down there, in addition to the kitchen that's on the second floor."

It was remarkable to me to realize that I'd lived in Vancouver my entire life and until today I'd never been inside a Vancouver Special. Ellie had clearly been inside at least one and knew the layout much better than I did.

"How do you know that?"

She rolled her eyes and took a sip of wine. "I have a client who is an architect. He can be interesting, although sometimes a little boring, and he tells me all kinds of stuff about the architecture of the city. Plus, I have a friend who has one in Marpole."

"So you think that Olivia might be hiding Emma on the

ground floor?" I paused in my chopping and reflected on the before-school chaos in the upstairs kitchen with Mrs. Tan, her children, and either her mother or her mother-in-law. "I suppose it's possible," I said. "Although Olivia seems like a law-abiding citizen, if you know what I mean. She doesn't exactly strike me as the rebellious type."

"Just a thought," Ellie said.

"Every thought is welcome." I pulled some lamb out of the fridge to chop up for curry. "It's worth following up. Thank you for mentioning that. I'll try to talk to Olivia again. Maybe I won't ask her the question directly, but I'll start hinting around and see if she shows her hand at all."

"Why don't you just come out and ask her?"

"It's kind of a gut feeling," I said, almost to myself. "I get the feeling that if I ask directly, I might spook Olivia, if that's actually what's going on."

Ellie made a gun with her right hand, her index finger pointing toward me. Then she dropped her thumb and made a clicking noise with her mouth. "Smarty," she said. "That's why you're doing this and not me. I'd just storm in there and start asking questions."

She wasn't wrong. This was a pretty astute assessment of herself. Ellie wasn't one for beating around the bush.

"Staying for supper?" I asked as I pulled out a large pot and put it on the stove.

"Yum. Yes, please." Ellie paused, crunching another carrot. "What do you think about Justin's family's grow-op? Could that be connected to Emma's disappearance?"

"I don't know. Justin's mother and dad were definitely on edge while I was there, but that could be due to other illegal stuff they might be up to. Unlike Olivia, they didn't seem to be the straight and narrow type."

I tossed some chopped onion and garlic into the pot and began stirring it around. I added the chunks of lamb and let them brown. Later I would add coconut milk and spices and vegetables. While I cooked, Ellie and I continued to talk over the elements of Emma's disappearance. Unfortunately, we didn't come up with any new ideas other than Ellie's theory about the ground floor of Olivia's house.

I kept the information about Emma's alleged contraband cell phone to myself. I knew that whatever I said, Ellie would naturally share with Laura. I had no problem with that; Laura deserved to know everything that was going on. But the cell phone issue was something that was not based in fact yet. I was simply taking Justin's word for it, and I knew from personal experience, from having been a thirteen-year-old myself many moons ago, that fact and fiction often got blurred when we were tweens. Stories got exaggerated; elements could become combined or separated very easily, and I knew that hyperbole was the second language of the ninth-grader.

So I sat on that information, feeling slightly guilty, but I also had a plan for finding out more about that phone. And I would be able to do it first thing the following morning.

Chapter 11

The police station where my friend Mack works is a six-story building near the entrance to the Cambie Street bridge. Cambie Street is a major north–south corridor through the city of Vancouver, and as it reaches Broadway, which is the east–west corridor, it slopes down a hill and becomes a bridge that spans the inlet called False Creek, which divides the downtown from the rest of the city. The police station is a nondescript building, and you wouldn't notice it unless you knew it was there. Other than the squad cars parked illegally in the alley behind it (oh, the irony) and also lined up in legal parking spots across the front, it looks like any other low-rise commercial building in the city.

I had set my alarm for 4 AM. Long before the sun was up, it bleeped at me and I was jerked out of a dream that, seconds later, I couldn't remember. I made myself swing my legs over the edge of the bed and sit up before I turned the alarm off, knowing that if I had just reached over and silenced it, I would have fallen immediately back to sleep. But the person that I wanted to see that morning kept odd hours, working nights rather than days, and I knew I'd have to be early to catch her as she left work. At least, that was my plan.

Dressed, coffee-d, and nearly awake, I pointed Loretta Jetta east along my sleepy street, driving past the community center where the outdoor pool used to be and over to Yukon Street. I hung a right, crossed 12th Avenue, then Broadway, and then found a parking space close to, but not too close to, the police precinct. Given the hour, I lucked out and found a spot half a block down from the exit to the parking garage. I sat and hugged my thermos cup and waited.

While I waited, my mind ticked over the information I had gathered the day before. Recapping with Ellie had been a big help, not that I thought I was any closer to figuring out where Emma was. But this morning I was a little more optimistic that I might be able to get closer to that goal, if I found the person I was looking for.

Up ahead, I could see where Cambie Street dipped and then rose, becoming a ramp to the bridge. It was still dark out and the sun wouldn't be up for another couple of hours. The vehicle traffic was light when I arrived, but got heavier as I waited.

My patience was rewarded. At 6:15, a figure came up out of the parking garage ramp wearing a helmet and reflective vest, riding a bicycle. I watched her reach up and flick on the headlamp on her helmet and then turn right out of the driveway.

As she came toward me, I jumped out of my car and trotted across the street. "Jane!" I was afraid she might not hear me if she had earbuds in, but again I lucked out. She stopped her bike and set one foot on the ground, peering at me in the pre-dawn light and the fuzzy glow of street lamps. I hoped I didn't look too threatening, coming at her out of nowhere.

Jane Bower and I had met several times through my friend Mack. They were coworkers and friends, and we often crossed paths at the barbecues and dinner parties that Mack and his husband John held regularly. Jane was tartly funny, with an acerbic wit that was lightning fast. She had a lifelong interest in sailing, and I thought she kept a small sailboat at a marina somewhere in North Van. She lived with a Great Dane named Monty, whose coat was spotted white and black like a Holstein cow. He usually accompanied Jane to Mack and John's dinner parties, arriving in style in the passenger seat of Jane's VW bug, looking like he was being driven around by his chauffeur. Jane worked in the police IT department and, according to legend, should she ever decide to go over to the dark side, her hacking skills had the potential to net her tenfold what she was making as a public servant.

I could see her squinting at me in the semi-darkness. "Freddie?"

"I'm glad I caught you…"

"What are you doing here at the crack of stupid?"

At Mack and John's dinners, Jane usually spent the evening talking to just one or two people; I, by contrast, would circulate, talking to as many people as I could, enjoying the noise and chatter. Jane had a limited capacity for that. She and Monty were usually gone by 8:30 or 9 PM, whereas Mack and John had to practically throw me out onto the street when it was time for them to go to bed. As an artist who worked alone much of the time, I got my people fixes wherever I could. Jane was the polar opposite to this, and it was reflected in her working life. She preferred to work nights, when it was quiet in the precinct.

I answered her question with a question. "I'm wondering if I could ask you a favor?"

Her eyes narrowed slightly. "You can ask," she said, typically concise and direct.

I responded by being equally direct, which I hoped she would appreciate. "I'm helping a friend whose child has gone missing. And I'm wondering if I could ask for your help to trace a cell phone number."

She hesitated, but her expression didn't change. Then she said, "You need a warrant to trace a telephone number."

"I know. And honestly, that's why I'm here asking you instead of Mack."

"If you don't have a warrant, Freddie, then I can't help you."

"My friend's daughter is thirteen. She's been missing for three days and her mother is frantic."

"Has the mother filed a missing persons report?"

"No. She seems to have a fear of the police."

Jane nodded. She was a woman working in a hierarchical culture that was male dominated, so she didn't need me to explain that to her a second time. But she started to shake her head again. I leapt in.

"She's thirteen, Jane. She's extremely smart. She loves to learn. She's a good kid. She's all her mother's got. She's an only child. They're barely scraping by."

My sob story didn't seem to have much of an effect on her. Jane pursed her lips, so I kept going. "What if it was Martin that was missing?"

Jane's eyes suddenly registered empathy, quickly followed by irritation. This was below the belt and I knew it. Like me, Jane didn't have children. Martin was her only nephew. And he was the light of her life. "That's not fair, Freddie."

"I know it's not, and I know it's illegal for you to do what I'm asking, but I also know that you can cover your tracks so that no one will ever know. I wouldn't ask if I thought it would get you in trouble."

"Get me fired, you mean."

I didn't answer. This was the moment to just keep my mouth shut and let her make a decision.

I could see Jane thinking. She glanced away from me, looking up ahead at the road that would lead her home. Finally, she turned back to me, her face still hardened, and my heart dropped. She was going to refuse me.

"Fine. I'll do it this once. But if you ever tell anyone anything about this, I will link your identity to a terrorist group and you'll never travel out of the country again without a cavity search."

"Deal," I said.

MOST OF JANE's colleagues work during the day. In the main part of the building, there would be officers up and about at this hour, finishing out their graveyard shifts, but Jane was one of the only ones who did that in the IT department. She turned her bike around and I gave her the phone number that Justin had given me. She didn't want me going into the building with her because the security cameras would record our every move. I agreed and went back and sat in my car, which I had positioned away from the building for just such an eventuality. She disappeared back into the bowels of the building and I sat sipping lukewarm coffee and praying to the patron saint of missing children to protect Jane and not let her get caught.

Thirty minutes went by, then forty-five, then an hour. I started to fret, thinking Jane had been caught and that I'd ruined her life.

Finally, she emerged back out of the parking garage ramp and turned right again, headed toward home. I caught a subtle jerk of her head as she passed me, an indication that I should follow her. I waited briefly and then started Loretta's engine and did a U-turn. A block and a half later I found Jane stopped, standing by her bike, waiting for me. I pulled up beside her and stopped. Given that Loretta Jetta was in her advancing years, I couldn't just roll down the automatic window on the passenger side. I hopped out and went around to Jane, who handed me a piece of paper.

"I never saw you. I don't know anything about this. And like I said, if you tell anyone…"

"I know, I know. Cavity searches. Thank you, Jane. I appreciate it so much. If I can ever do anything for you, just call me."

Her expression softened. "I might need a date to my cousin's wedding next summer."

I smiled at her, knowing I'd been forgiven. She knew I was straight, but I'd occasionally caught her eyes following me at Mack and John's parties. "I'm your girl," I said. "Just tell me when and where."

I was rewarded with a small smile, and then she hopped up on her bike and rode away.

Chapter 12

Even though I'd been up for hours it was still only 7 AM. I was hungry. I took myself back into my neighborhood and went to my favorite kitschy breakfast place. It was an extremely popular spot, but I was so early that I managed to get a seat. I sat at a small table for two and placed my order for eggs Benny and hash browns and then pulled out my phone and the piece of paper that Jane had given me.

The paper had three things on it: a name, an address, and a phone number different than the one I'd gotten from Justin. I studied the address and realized it was about two blocks away from Emma's school. On my phone I pulled up a browser and searched for the name on the paper. Unfortunately, the name was Mike Williams, one of the most generic names on the planet. Facebook had dozens of Mike Williamses in Vancouver alone, and none of the other social media outlets were particularly helpful either. My breakfast arrived and I set the paper and my phone aside and tucked in.

I wasn't sure what the name on the paper could mean. I assumed the information meant that the phone was registered to this person, but if that was the case, why did Emma have it? Did she know him? Was he the friend from school Justin had vaguely referenced? Maybe he was someone that Laura knew. I thought about asking her, but decided not to just yet. I didn't want to frighten her unnecessarily if she didn't know the guy. I tried to enjoy my meal, but I was anxious to get going so I paid the bill as soon as I was finished and headed back over to Laura and Emma's neighborhood.

I CRUISED SLOWLY past the address on Jane's piece of paper and saw that it was a small, stuccoed bungalow set back further from the street than most houses on the block. The front yard was bare soil, not grass. In the dirt I could see dormant grooves spaced evenly apart that in the summer would be filled with growth. The yard had been converted to a vegetable garden.

This had become more popular across the city lately for two reasons. The first was the increasing appeal of eating locally and sustainably. The second was that Vancouver lawns had started to become infested with little critters called chafer beetles, which feasted on the roots of grass lawns. Gradually a lawn would turn brown as the grass died as a result of being eaten from below, and then the infestation would spread down the block. But, interestingly, the beetles were not interested in the roots of other plants, like vegetables. Many front yards in my own neighborhood had been turned into kitchen gardens as well. The beetles hadn't hit my block yet, but it was likely only a matter of time. When they arrived, I'd likely adopt a similar strategy. I'd always had a secret urge to live closer to the land. Not an easy thing to do in a metropolis, of course, but perhaps a few rows of green beans and lettuce could change that for me.

It took me some time to find a parking space, as it always does in Vancouver, but eventually I found one that was mostly legal. I walked back toward the little bungalow, wondering what my approach was going to be. I was making the assumption that the place belonged to this Mike Williams, whoever he was. I decided that maybe I would bluff my way in the door, whatever that meant, and then see where things went.

My heart was beating faster than it normally does, and I had a serious case of butterflies in my stomach. But I went up the front walk like I knew what I was doing and knocked at the door. It opened, and my eyes dropped to a girl who looked to be about six years old, her blonde hair tied back in a ponytail and the area around her mouth smeared with jam. For the second time in two days I was interrupting a family's breakfast. I heard an adult call out from inside the house.

"Who is it?"

The girl looked at me directly and took a bite of the piece of toast that was in her right hand. "Who are you?" she said, chewing.

From behind her, a woman with the same corn-silk blonde hair and blue eyes appeared. "Can I help you?"

Now it was time for the bluffing. "I'm here to see Mike."

"Oh, sure," she said, and then turned to walk back into the house, calling, "Mike! Someone's here for you."

The girl followed her mom and the two of them disappeared into the house. I stood on the doorstep, not quite knowing what to do. But not too much time went by before a man came down the hallway in front of me carrying a child who was mostly asleep and looked to be maybe a year old. The man was a little shorter than me, so that probably made him about 5' 7". He was well padded everywhere, just on the cusp of being chubby. His fair hair was receding, and he had a pretty serious widow's peak. He had a gentle and open expression on his face, which helped calm the butterflies in my stomach.

He came toward me and said, "Are you Michelle?"

I decided I couldn't bluff that much. "No, I'm Freddie. I

wanted to ask you about a phone you might have given to a girl named Emma."

"Oh, sure. Come on in."

He held one arm out in a welcoming way and I stepped inside while he closed the front door behind me. The child in his arms stuck his thumb in his mouth and pushed his forehead deeper into his father's neck. Mike unconsciously patted the boy's back and said, "Come with me. We're just feeding everybody breakfast. You know what the morning routine is like."

I didn't, not being a parent myself, but I didn't say that to him. The six-year-old was sitting at a kitchen table that was nestled against one wall of the smallish kitchen. As I followed Mike into the room, he handed the younger child to his wife and she settled him into a high chair. Mike waved toward another seat at the table.

"Have a seat. Would you like some coffee?"

I accepted. I'd already had too much coffee that day, but it seemed like the polite thing to do.

The adults bustled around for a few moments and I stayed quiet, letting them get on with their routine. I had the sense that they would get settled shortly and be able to focus on me, and that turned out to be the case. From the high chair, the toddler watched me with solemnity, working away on his thumb, his eyelids droopy. Mike poured coffee for the three adults in the room and put a couple of pieces of bread in the toaster. His wife, whose name I learned was Merrin, sat down beside the high chair and started attempting to spoon orange mush into the baby's mouth. Much of it got smeared on his face or was spat out again. He didn't seem as interested in eating as he was in staring at me.

The girl, who was kneeling on the chair beside me, had her toast in one hand and a small plastic horse figurine in the other. She was walking the horse around the table and murmuring to herself.

"What's the horse's name?" I asked her.

"Butterfly," she said, quietly.

"Does Butterfly eat toast for breakfast too?"

"Nooo," she groaned, in a tone that implied this question was ridiculous. "She eats magic corn and sausages. They help her to fly." She lifted the horse off the table and sailed it though the air.

The toast popped. Mike buttered and jammed it and then sat down with a little sigh in a chair beside his wife. Reflexively, he rested his right hand on her back and then took a bite of toast. While he chewed, he turned to me.

"Okay," he said with a deep breath. "How can we help you?"

"So, you know Emma Reid?"

"Sure," he nodded. "She's my math star."

Ah—so he was one of Emma's teachers. That piece slotted into place in my head. "I'm not sure if you've heard, but she went missing a few days ago."

Mike's jaw stopped working momentarily, and Merrin glanced over at me with horrified eyes.

"No," Mike said. "Really?"

"I'm afraid so."

He and Merrin and the toddler were all now staring at me. Butterfly's mistress was unconcerned and continued talking quietly to herself about their adventures.

Mike finally said, "I noticed she hadn't been in class, but the office said she was sick. What happened?"

This slowed me down for a second. Had the office been telling the teachers Emma was sick? If so, had that information come from Laura? I'd have to check. "That's what I'm trying to find out. Emma's mother is a little anxious about going to the police, so she's asked me to see if I can find Emma for her."

"Okaaay." There was note of skepticism in his voice, but

then he carried on. "We'll do anything we can help, won't we, hon?" He glanced at his wife and she nodded.

"Was Emma at math club last Tuesday?" I asked.

Mike nodded and took another bite of toast.

"I understand that Emma has a cell phone that might be registered to you. Were you aware of this?"

"For sure. I set that up for her a few months ago." He seemed very matter-of-fact about it, as though it was perfectly normal for a teacher to give a student a phone.

I waited for him to explain, but he seemed to be waiting for me, so I asked, "Is that something you normally do for your students?"

Mike took another bite of toast and a sip of coffee. "No, of course not." He chewed and swallowed. "Emma is my superstar, you see. No matter what I throw at her, she learns it more quickly and more thoroughly than any of the other kids, even though everyone else in the club is brilliant. I'm not supposed to say this, but she's my favorite kid in math club. And I think she knows it. Anyway, she came to me one day and said she had heard that I refurbish old phones. It's a hobby of mine. Keeps them out of the landfill, and sometimes I sell them online."

The toddler started to kick his tiny feet against the high chair and talk to his mother very seriously in a language all his own. She continued trying to coax his breakfast into him.

"Did Emma have a specific reason for wanting the phone?"

Mike shrugged and took another sip of coffee. "Not really. I sort of guessed it was just the old peer pressure thing. She's thirteen. All her friends have phones."

I thought all this over for a second, taking a sip of coffee myself. Mike seemed utterly unperturbed by what he'd done, but it didn't seem normal to me. It felt to me like he had crossed a professional boundary with Emma, and I wasn't comfortable with the whole scenario. My concern must have shown up on my face, because Merrin spoke up.

"It sounds a little weird, doesn't it?" she said, taking a break from trying to push more orange goo into her younger child. "A teacher giving a student a phone. But there's nothing weird about it, I promise you, Ms...."

"Lark," I said. "But you can call me Freddie."

Merrin continued. "I promise you there's nothing weird about it, Freddie. Mike's just a good guy who wants to help everyone when he can." She glanced at her husband with warm eyes. The honeymoon was clearly not over for these two, even with two young children.

I didn't have the same faith in her husband, though. Not that I thought he was a pedophile, but I'd only known him for ten minutes and the whole thing did seem odd to me. I looked back at Mike. "Laura, Emma's mom, isn't aware of the phone." This fact wasn't helping his case with me.

For the first time, he looked the tiniest bit chagrined. "You're right. I didn't clear it with Laura. Emma asked me not to. She said her mom didn't agree with kids having phones, but that she, Emma, was tired of not being able to text her friends."

"And the phone is still registered to you, right? That means the bill comes to you?"

"Yeah, that's right. Emma does the best she can to pay the bill every month. I told her it was twenty dollars, and she saves up her babysitting money and gives that to me each month. Of course, the bill is more than that, but I just make up the difference."

I was still having a difficult time accepting this at face value.

I was about to say something when Merrin spoke up again. She had given up on the orange goo and had handed the baby a slice of banana that he was now smearing between his hands and all over the tray of his high chair.

"I promise you, Freddie, Mike's not a weirdo. He's not grooming Emma for anything. He's just a good guy who cares about his students and happens to also be a total electronics nerd. Mike knew that he could give Emma a cheap phone. Something that she was really wanting and something that would make her feel like she fit in with the other kids." She glanced at her husband and then continued. "I gather from what Mike says that that's something she doesn't feel very often. She can't afford the same kind of clothes the other kids wear. She and her mom never go on the vacations that the other kids in the school go on. Sometimes her mom can't afford to send Emma on school trips, and either the school chips in for her or Emma has to stay back and spend the day in the library by herself. So he genuinely was just trying to do something nice for someone he cares about."

Merrin's explanation was certainly heartfelt, and I could tell that she really believed what she was saying, but I took it all with a very large grain of salt.

The toddler was getting more and more restless, straining to get out of his high chair, pressing up with his little arms, lifting his bum off the seat and making squeaking noises. Beside me, the girl said, "Can we go to the park now?" She looked at her mom when she said it, but I felt the message was directed at me. It was my cue to leave the family to their Saturday.

I thanked them and stood up. Mike walked me to the front door and told me to let him know if I had any other questions. From the back of the house came a shriek, then the sounds of the toddler crying. Mike glanced over his shoulder as he opened the door for me. I started to say goodbye, but he was walking back down the hall. I let myself out and closed the door behind me.

Chapter 13

I needed comfort.

Things were changing quickly. Just two days earlier, I'd been an artist with a penchant for dark chocolate, a slight phobia about clowns, and far too many pairs of dangly turquoise earrings. Now I found myself stalking teenagers, discovering possibly illegal pot-growing operations, and asking acquaintances to break the law at their places of work.

I needed the unspoken reassurance that came with being around close friends. So I got myself an invitation to dinner at my friend Mack's house.

It wasn't hard.

I texted his husband and said, "Can I come for dinner?" He responded yes and gave me specific instructions about what kind of wine to bring, which I was more than happy to do.

Mack and John live in Dunbar, close to the edge of Pacific Spirit Park, a forested area with walking trails nearly three times the size of New York's Central Park on the far west edge of Vancouver. They bought the house years ago and have been slowly renovating and improving it. The layout is much the same as mine, with a kitchen at the back that looks out onto a large backyard with tons of privacy in the form of several huge maple trees. In the autumn, the two men spend half their waking hours raking the leaves, of course, but John swears it's worth it. They built a big deck off the kitchen with steps that lead down onto another seating area where, in good weather, they host barbecues. John loves to cook and looks for any excuse to do so.

We wouldn't be sitting on the deck tonight, though. It was raining again and likely wouldn't stop until April. I arrived at the front door, wine in hand, and let myself in.

"Hello? I'm here."

"Come on back," I heard John yell.

I grew up with John's husband, James 'Mack' McCormack. We had lived on the same block in this very neighborhood, and our parents had socialized together. He was more like a cousin or a brother than a friend. The only thing Mack had ever wanted to do in life was to be a police officer, and he had accomplished that with few bumps in the road. By the time he was twenty-six, he had a master's degree in criminology from Simon Fraser University. He had been accepted into the police academy the following September and had sailed through the training.

On this particular Saturday night, we ate a beautiful lamb roast with potatoes and carrots that John had prepared. Somehow, he was able to whip these things up without any notice at all. There was salad and even pie that he had pulled out of the freezer.

Throughout the meal, however, I found myself distracted, losing the thread of the conversation, worrying about Emma and Laura. I felt out of my depth and more than a little ridiculous, like I was playing cops and robbers. Except I had a paintbrush, not a gun. The worst part was that I couldn't tell Mack, my closest friend, even a whisper of what was going on. If I had, he would have not only admonished me but likely put me under house arrest. Besides, Laura had made abundantly clear that she wanted to keep the situation away from the police.

Bellies full, Mack and I cleaned the kitchen while John watched a Canucks game in the living room. The deal in their house was that whoever cooked didn't have to clean up.

"You're quiet tonight," Mack said as he scrubbed the roasting pan.

"Am I?" I was drying a wine glass. "Just thoughtful, I guess."

"Thoughtful about what?"

I avoided his question by asking one of my own. "Why did you join the police force?"

He glanced at me, his bare forearms submerged in the sink. "That's an odd question after all these years."

"Humor me."

"Well," he began. His scrubbing motions slowed as he thought. "It's the only thing I ever wanted to do, I suppose. I remember telling my art teacher in grade seven that I was going to be a cop. He was horrified."

"Really?"

"Yeah. He was a bit of a counter-culture guy. Thought the police were Nazis."

"But you didn't see it that way."

"No."

I thought he was going to say something else, but he was quiet, so I asked, "What did you see that appealed to you at such a young age?"

Mack lifted the roasting pan out of the sink and examined it. "Remember Mr. Rankin, who lived on the next block over from us?"

This was unexpected. I thought back but couldn't picture him. "Nope."

"He drove a dark green Mustang Fastback."

I shook my head.

Mack was quiet for a moment and then said, "At

Hallowe'en he always had a recording of spooky noises playing on his porch and several pumpkins carved, not just one or two."

I could picture the house now. "And he had a boxer dog named Daisy."

"That's him. Well, he was a cop."

"Was he?"

"Yeah. And I thought he was the coolest dude going. Way cooler than my dad. That car he drove?" Mack made a slightly sexual, yearning sound. "To me he was Steve Austin and Superman rolled into one."

"Who's Steve Austin?"

"The Six Million Dollar Man."

"Oh, right."

"Anyway, something about him captured my attention." Mack rinsed the roasting pan and put it in the draining tray, ready for me to dry. "I used to ride by his house on my bike every day to see if he was outside. And when he was, I'd pepper him with questions about being a cop. He loved it."

"Your questions?"

Mack made a small snorting noise. "No, I think those were just annoying, though he was very patient with me. He loved being a cop. He said there was nothing like it, and he took the job very seriously. Anyway," he glanced around looking to see if he'd missed washing anything, "that was it. It was like falling in love. From then on, there was no other profession for me."

I thought about this, relating it to my own drive to make art, something that I'd felt very early on. "But what was it, specifically, about being a cop that attracted you?"

"You mean like the uniform or the guns or something?" He began wiping off the island.

"More than that. The essence of it."

He snorted again. "Well, now you're getting too deep for me. I'm just a guy who thinks he looks sexy in the dress blues."

"Yes!" John yelled from the living room, but not about Mack's uniform. It appeared the Canucks had scored a goal.

The moment was over. Mack left the kitchen to see the replay, and I finished drying the pots and pans and putting them away. His words stayed with me, though.

Mack's moral compass pointed toward justice. Maybe he wouldn't put it in those terms, but I suspected that's what had called him to be a police officer. Righting wrongs. And that was the same thing that was drawing me to continue to help Laura despite my early reluctance. I didn't fully understand why she didn't want to tell the police what had happened, but I knew if I planned to continue to help her, I'd have to respect that and work around it.

I gave the counter one last swipe with the dishcloth, my heart and mind somewhat easier.

When I left, I gave both men a big hug, which was normal, but John noticed that I held on to him for a second or two longer than usual.

"Everything okay, Fred?" John was the only person allowed to call me Fred.

I gave him a little extra squeeze. "All good. I'm just grateful for you guys."

They shifted on their feet and made mild jokes, uncomfortable with my sudden sentimentality. I held the Tupperware container they'd given me, filled with lamb and vegetables, and trotted through the rain to my car, both wishing I didn't have to leave and also buoyed and ready to face what might come.

Chapter 14

It was just after 10 PM when I got home. The space that had originally been allocated for a garage on my small city lot was now being occupied by the laneway house that Ellie rented. So I tended to park on the street, as so many Vancouverites do. I was usually pretty lucky finding a spot close to the house, but tonight I had to park half a block away. I was yawning and looking forward to a better night's sleep than I'd had the night before.

I turned onto my front walk, making a mental list of what I would do the next day, including going back to the Tans' to see what the situation was in their ground-level suite and whether Olivia could be hiding Emma somewhere in their house. I was automatically and absentmindedly digging through my purse for my house keys when I felt rather than saw a presence come up behind me. For a second, I thought it might be Blythe, but then I realized there were two people, one on either side of me. I started to turn my head to the right when huge hands grabbed both of my upper arms and lifted me up off the ground. I dropped Mack and John's leftover container as I was propelled forward and up the four small steps to my front door. I barely even had time to be shocked before one of my attackers grabbed the keys out of my hand and unlocked the door. They pushed me inside and closed the door behind me, dropping the keys on the floor. Then once again, they lifted me up and sped me forward into the living room. My tippy-toes barely touched the floor as they rushed me over and threw me into an upholstered chair on one side of the room beside the old fireplace.

Other than light from the street, the room was dark. One of the men who had manhandled me walked to the front of the room where there was a standing lamp and turned it on. Now I had a clearer view of who I was dealing with. There were three men, not just two.

The two men who had carried me in were built like bouncers—tall and overly muscular in a way that showed that they were trying too hard. One of them was bald, and the other one had a short, marine drill sergeant haircut. They were both dressed in black T-shirts, black cargo pants and black lace-up army-style boots.

The third man was dressed in a dark gray suit with a pale blue silk tie that looked like it might have white polka dots on it. He looked very pleased with himself as we sized each other up. He was shorter than the two musclemen, but not by much. His hair was longish and swept back in a style that I abhorred on men. He had an attractive, if slightly asymmetrical, face and hard eyes.

The suit was what made the man, in this case. It likely cost far more than the average monthly rent in Vancouver, which was saying something. It fit his tall, slender frame like it had been made for him, which I was positive it had been. White cuffs poked out a perfect length from his jacket sleeves. His pocket square wasn't the same design as his tie, but it compli-mented it perfectly. He looked impeccable, and he knew it. I've had that feeling occasionally, when a dress fitted me perfectly and I was at a weight I was feeling smug about. It had been a fleeting feeling for me. For this guy, it looked like he lived in that zone. I would have bet money he had six other suits at home that fit him just as well. Where the bodyguards were protected by their muscles, Gray Suit was wearing his armor in the form of sartorial superiority.

There was a three- or four-second gap after I landed in the chair while Gray Suit and I sized one another up. Then I said, "Did your mommy buy you that tie?"

The urge to be sarcastic and belittling was instinctive. It was my armor. I was pissed off for any number of reasons, but highest on my list was the fact that I didn't know what in the holy hell was going on. And, of course, I was terrified.

I was pretty certain that it would take only a few minutes before I'd figure out why they were here. I ran through a list of the valuables in my house and didn't come up with much. Walter and Stella had raised my sister and me not to be very consumerist, and as a result I was something of a minimalist. The most valuable room in my house was probably the art studio, and that only because of all the money I'd spent on paint and canvases and other painting equipment. I didn't own a lot of expensive jewelry or have pricey knickknacks around the house. The things that were valuable to me in that house were sentimental rather than having any market value.

Gray Suit looked at me and smirked. "You're a smart-ass. I like that. We'll see how smart you are before we leave."

The exchange reminded me of when I occasionally bumped into raccoons in the back alley. There was an intelligence there behind his eyes, but there was also an awareness and calculation that I wasn't comfortable with.

I settled into the chair, straightening my spine, refusing to cower or let on how terrified I was. The two bodyguards stood sentry on either side of Gray Suit, expressionless, staring at me.

Gray Suit's head had been swiveling around, taking in the room and the dining room / office beyond that. He took his time about it. Controlling the room with his energy. Finally, his head swiveled back to me. The look in his eyes was scarier than the two thugs on either side of him, combined.

"You're going to stop looking for Emma Reid," he said. He said it without any kind of aggression or hostility. It was simply a fact, as though he had said, "I'm going to buy tomatoes at the grocery store."

The part of my brain that wasn't freaking out went *Huh. Interesting.*

"Am I?" I said. "Why is that?"

Gray Suit gave a little smirk and glanced at one of his compatriots and then back at me. "Because I said so."

"And who are you?"

"I am your worst nightmare," he said.

A big guffaw burst out of my chest. It was such a cliché, like something from a Bruce Willis movie.

He didn't like that. His face hardened even further, but all he said was, "Richard."

The bodyguard on his left took two steps over to the fireplace. On the mantel there was a brightly colored porcelain vase that I had brought back from a trip to Portugal, a photo of my family from when I was about nine, two ceramic candlesticks that I'd made, and a glass bird that Blythe had brought me from a trip to Venice. Without a word and without hesitating, the bodyguard picked the bird off the mantel. He pivoted, like an outfielder retrieving a baseball off the wall and turning to throw to second base. And just like that outfielder, he threw the bird, baseball style, at the opposite wall of the living room. It smashed into a framed painting. The glass in the frame shattered, as did the bird, spraying shards outward, like a fountain. The painting came off the wall and crash-landed onto the back of the couch below it and then slid down between the couch and wall, crunching loudly.

The sudden noise and violence were clearly deliberate. I was shocked, naturally, and even more frightened than I had been, but I tried desperately not to show it. I met Gray Suit's eyes and held them and, with a tremendous amount of restraint, didn't say a word. I didn't cry or flinch or allow myself any kind of reaction. I just stared at him. Gray Suit held my eyes in a mini-staring contest for a few seconds.

And then that was it. To my surprise, he turned, walked back toward the front door, and left. The bodyguards followed him and suddenly I was alone in the room again.

I walked over to the front window, crunching through glass and grinding it into the area rug in the middle of the room. I watched while the three men climbed into an enormous black SUV that was at least as large as Ellie's. The two bodyguards got in the front seats and Gray Suit got in the back. I trotted over to the front door and bolted it shut. I picked up my keys from where they lay and put them in the dish by the front door where I always kept them.

Then, I heard the back door open. I froze, wondering if the men had just gone around into the alley and were coming back in again for some more fun and games. But then I heard Ellie's voice.

"Freddie? Are you okay? I heard an almighty crash."

I walked down the hallway to the kitchen at the back of the house and straight into Ellie's arms. She wrapped those strong arms around me and held me without a word as I sobbed.

Chapter 15

When Ellie had mopped me up, dried my tears, and helped me to quiet down, we took a look at the damage in the living room. She got me to walk through the whole story and I remembered a few extra details while I did that. Things like the fact that Gray Suit had worn a gold pinky ring on his left hand. And the bodyguard with the bald head had a horizontal scar on his chin.

Ellie listened to me silently, her face frozen in shock. When I finished, she gave me another hug and said simply, "Bastards."

We pulled the couch out and got a broom and the vacuum and started to clean up. The painting canvas that had been in the frame was undamaged, but the glass was destroyed, of course. It wasn't one of my own paintings; it was by one of my favorite artists from Quebec, and it could be re-framed. The glass bird, however, would not live to see another day. This made me so sad, because it had been a gift from my sister. We swept up all the shards and vacuumed furiously, but even so, weeks later I would still be finding tiny pieces of glass in odd places in the living room.

When we were done, we pushed the couch back to its original position against the wall and Ellie put the kettle on to make us both a cup of tea. I sat at the one of the stools at the kitchen island and let her organize things. I noticed my body was shaking on the inside, like I was cold. I felt shattered myself, like the bird, and small.

It had all been so easy for the three men. Whoever they were, they had just come up behind me and marched me into my house—practically carried me. I had no idea who they were or how they'd found me.

Ellie sat down on the barstool beside me.

I wrapped my hands around the warm cup of tea, grateful for its comfort. "I have to get Mack involved now," I said.

Ellie took a sip of her tea and then set the mug down on the counter. "I know this has been terrible. It's just an awful thing that's happened to you and you must feel so frightened, honey. But I wonder if I could ask you something?" She carried on without waiting for me to assent. "I wonder if you'd be willing to come with me and talk to Laura before you talk to Mack. There's something you should know."

Ellie's face was serious, which was a dramatic departure from her normal expression. There was always a bit of the performer about Ellie, no matter what the situation. She liked to live in the spotlight, whether there was one pointed at her or not. Her personality was huge, and she was funny and bright. I always enjoyed being around her in a group setting because I could just sit back and enjoy the show.

At that moment, sitting at my kitchen island, I'd known Ellie for roughly three and a half years, and this was the first time I'd ever seen her so still and quiet. Her arms weren't gesticulating. Her bracelets weren't jangling. Whatever the reason that she wanted me to talk to Laura before I went to Mack, it must be a good one.

I nodded and took a sip of my tea.

~

THE NEXT MORNING, Laura's apartment was in about the same state as it had been two days before when I had first met her. The same rumpled blankets on the couch. The same dishes filling the kitchen sink. The same funk of cigarette smoke and grief.

Ellie had let me sleep on her couch the night before. There was no way I was staying in my house alone. In the morning, she had called Laura to say we were on our way over, and had had to quickly put in that we weren't coming with any good news but that we needed to speak to her. The disappointment in Laura's voice had been palpable. Now in the apartment, Ellie sat on the couch beside Laura while she chain-smoked. I picked up the same aged dining room chair I'd sat in before and turned it so that I could face them both.

There was something going on between Ellie and Laura. I could see it as soon as we sat down. Ellie was still out of her performance mode. She sat close to Laura but not touching her. As she began explaining to her what had happened at my house, I watched Laura's face. At the very start of the story, Laura looked uninterested and preoccupied. But as Ellie described the events, and the people involved, her expression changed. She had been sitting slumped back into the couch, made of wet noodles, but as the story progressed her eyes widened slightly. She pulled her bare feet up under her and sat cross-legged, her whole body coming into high alert. When Ellie finished, Laura's face had settled into an expression of resignation, fear, and something akin to bitterness.

As Ellie told the story, she checked a few facts with me, but she had it all down pretty well. When she finished, we were all quiet for a moment, and then Ellie said, "Do you want to tell Freddie or do you want me to?"

"I will," Laura said. "It's only fair." She reached forward, grabbed her cigarette pack off the table, and lit one with a shaking hand. When she'd taken a drag, she looked at me and said, "This is the best and worst possible news."

I must have looked confused. "Why?"

Laura blew a stream of smoke out of a tightly pursed mouth. "Because now I know who took Emma."

GRAY SUIT AND HIS BODYGUARDS, Laura explained, were employees of Laura's ex-husband, Emma's father.

"How do you know?" I asked.

"I just do." She pulled on her cigarette again and then her chin began to wrinkle and her eyes filled with tears. "So what that means is that Emma hasn't run away and she hasn't been taken by some random stranger. And she's alive."

Ellie reached over and squeezed Laura's free hand, and Laura began to cry in earnest. The relief she felt must have been enormous. Three and a half days of not knowing where her child was, likely imagining the worst possible scenarios. Sleepless nights wondering if Emma was frightened, cold, hungry, or worse. I could see the release of all that tension and anguish rolling through Laura, like a wave cresting. She leaned forward, set her cigarette in the bowl of butts, and then bent her head over her lap and sobbed, her shoulders and back shaking. Ellie stood up and went to the bathroom, returning quickly with a box of tissues. She pulled three in rapid succession and handed them to Laura.

We sat quietly, letting Laura cry. My heart ached watching her. I had never been a parent, but given how much I loved my sister, and how it had felt to lose her, I could imagine something of what Laura was feeling.

When the storm had eased somewhat and Laura was collecting herself, Ellie begin to explain more of the details to me. "Laura's ex-husband, Chad, is a bad dude, shall we say. He's involved in all kinds of illegal businesses." Ellie had been looking at Laura, but now she looked over at me again.

Shivers ran down the backs of my arms. "So Chad is the guy in the gray suit?"

Laura blew her nose and shook her head. "That guy must be an employee." She took a deep breath. "Let me go back to the beginning. Chad and I met in Kelowna, where we had both grown up. We dated for a while and I was madly in love with him. He's very charismatic, and handsome. And incredibly smart. I was nineteen and I was swayed by things like the expensive jewelry that he bought me and the car that he drove." She took another breath, shoring herself up, it seemed. "I got pregnant. of course, because I was an idiot, but Chad was thrilled. He was so excited to start a family, and we moved in together right away. And got married." She gave a little resigned sigh.

"As soon as we moved in together, he began to change. He was still the same charming, charismatic, overly affectionate person. But he became more controlling, telling me what to wear and how to do my hair. At first, I took it as a compliment, that he cared about who I was. But then, as I grew more and more pregnant, he began to insult my body as well, calling me fat. Then at other times he was really great to me, and when we would go out for dinner with our friends, he would show me off and talk about what a great family we were going to be and how amazing I was. The whole time, he continued to shower me with gifts. His friends painted the nursery, and we bought the latest and greatest crib and stroller. But he was like two different people." She shrugged. "I didn't understand what was going on. One minute he was so great to me, and the next he was so vicious."

I listened and felt so sad for Laura. It was such a common story, and for the millionth time I wondered why men think it's okay to treat women in this way.

Laura continued her story, not looking at either Ellie or me, just staring, head lowered, at the coffee table. "Then Emma was born." Laura's eyes lit up for the first time since I'd known her. "She was just the best thing ever. And for a few weeks, Chad was normal. He was so good to me and so good to Emma, and it was like all the stuff that had gone on before hadn't happened. I couldn't believe it. I thought everything was fixed." Now her face fell. "It didn't last, of course. By the time Emma was about six weeks old, things had gone back to normal. He would blow up at the slightest thing. I was exhausted, and Emma was colicky, so I was awake most nights with her and then during the day as well. Chad couldn't stand the smell of sour breast milk, but Emma spit up constantly, of course, because she was a baby. And so," she took another deep breath, "he hit me. The first time we were both so shocked. I think he was just as surprised as I was." I doubted that, but I kept my mouth shut. "And he apologized like crazy afterwards, and swore it would never happen again. But it did." She shrugged again. "He always blamed it on me. If I could do better, if I could be different, if I was a better mother and a better wife, he wouldn't lose his temper. So it was my fault. I tried harder and harder, but nothing I ever did was enough."

My heart ached for Laura and for Emma. If I hadn't known that they were both still alive in this moment, I would've been terrified for them, wondering how the story was going to end.

"The one saving grace was that Chad always reserved his anger for me. He never went near Emma when he was in a mood." Laura paused, and I got the sense we had come to the climax of the story. "And then one day when Emma was about thirteen months old, Chad was in a rage. He was throwing things at me and hitting and kicking me in the living room. I can't even remember what set him off. I was so exhausted. But that was normal, and I was just dealing with it. And then he stormed off and went into Emma's room where she was sleeping." Laura's eyes were wide and still at the memory.

"I ran after him into her room and he was standing over her, furious. He picked her up out of the crib, just jerked her out of there." Laura made a little motion with her hands, not seeming to be aware of where she was. I was sure she was back in this horrifying moment. There were tears running down her face now, though she wasn't sobbing; she was telling the story very calmly. "Emma started to cry immediately, of course, because he jerked her right out of her sleep. Chad started shouting with her in his arms and shaking her. He said he would kill us both if things didn't change. I was screaming and crying and trying to get Emma out of his hands, but he wouldn't let her go. He was raging because he said I loved Emma more than I loved him. And that he would take care of that once and for all. And then he threw Emma back in her crib. I can still see her bouncing off the mattress, screaming and crying. He stormed out of the room and tried to punch me in the head on the way out, but I ducked away from him." She gave a bitter snort.

Laura stopped talking then, and the three of us sat quietly. Laura took a sip out of the mug in front of her.

Ellie picked up the thread of the story then, looking at me. "Laura had heard of the women's shelter in Kelowna, so she went there for help."

Laura carried on, wiping her face on the sleeves of her hoodie. "I had been thinking about it for a while, but of course I had talked myself out of it every time, thinking that I could somehow make him happy and things might change. And because he had never threatened Emma or gone anywhere near her, other than to play with her, I thought it was okay. If he was just directing his rage at me, then somehow Emma would be safe. But that day in her room changed everything. I knew I had to get out. He had stormed out of the house and sometimes he could be gone for two or three days. So I packed a few things in a small suitcase. You know, one of those carry-on-sized ones?" She looked at me.

I nodded.

"I got an few of Emma's things together. She was screaming the whole time, terrified. And we left. I put her in her stroller, still crying, and I had a knapsack on my back and the wheely suitcase. I didn't have a car, of course. Chad didn't let me have one. He said that when I needed to get around town, I could take the bus, even with a little kid." She stopped, and Ellie picked up the story again.

She explained that Chad was well known in Kelowna at that point for his criminal activities. So when Laura told the women at the shelter who he was, they knew they would have to do something extraordinary to keep her safe. So Laura entered what is referred to as the underground.

For the next little while, Laura and Ellie alternatively explained what had happened and how Laura and Emma had ended up in Vancouver. There was a network of women, many of them abuse survivors themselves, who would take in women who were on the run from their husbands or partners. They would help them find new places to live and set up new homes, and in many cases new identities.

Laura and Emma's names weren't the ones they had been born with. They had been given new identification. All of their ID was false, of course, but it was enough. Within 24 hours, they had been whisked away to Vancouver.

"I barely remember any of that next week or so," Laura said. "I just trusted that these women had my best interests at heart, and they did. They found us a tiny little basement suite just off Kingsway. And they found me my job at the library and subsidized daycare for Emma. And things have been great for a long time. Emma and I have a really good life."

She had been barely twenty when all of this had unfolded, Ellie said. So much for someone so young to handle. It was a lot for me to take in, and I couldn't even imagine the things that Laura had lived through—starting with the abuse by her husband. And the fact that she was sitting here in front of me in her little apartment, having raised a child who was by all accounts a lovely person, was a testament to Laura's strength and resilience.

When the story was done, the three of us sat quietly, privately thinking our own thoughts.

Eventually I asked, "Does Emma know any of this?"

Laura shook her head. "She was too young to remember any of the stuff before we left. And then as she got older, I just told her that her dad wasn't in the picture anymore. I thought about telling her he had died, but I didn't. She accepted what I'd said, the way kids do, and has never really had many questions. If she asks about him, I paint a picture of the good guy that I dated briefly before we got married. And I say we just couldn't be together, that his work took him away from us."

Outside, a car alarm started blaring and I realized that for the duration of Laura's story I had been in a bubble, not aware of where I was or the sounds and sights around me. It was such a horrifying story and yet so common, which made me sick to my stomach.

Despite how I felt, I had some follow-up questions. "Does Emma ask why her father doesn't try to see her?"

"She's asked that once or twice, and each time I've told her he left before she was born and that he'd never met her." Laura squirmed a little on the couch. She seemed uncomfortable, which was understandable. "I told her it was always just her and me, and that I had all the love she needed."

Another question occurred to me. "What about your parents?"

"We're not close." She made the bitter snort again. "To say the least. I lived in the basement guest room of a girlfriend's parents' house for my last two years of high school because my parents were so useless. Alcoholics, both of them."

"And you were an only child?"

Laura nodded.

I looked at Ellie. "And you're sure the man in the gray suit wasn't Chad?"

Ellie and Laura glanced at one another, and then Ellie looked back at me. "Yes. The way you describe him, it doesn't sound like Chad. But I am ninety-nine percent positive he must work for Chad."

I thought about this for a second. "So Chad sent them down from Kelowna?"

It was Laura who spoke up this time. "No. Chad is living in Vancouver now. I got word from one of the women in the shelter in Kelowna about three years ago that Chad had moved his operation down here."

Chapter 16

My mind was whirling, connecting the dots and filling in the blanks. "You think Chad has Emma."

"I'd bet my life on it," Laura said, bitterness creeping into her voice. "I don't know how he found her, but the appearance of those thugs at your house isn't a coincidence." She looked at Ellie and then at me. "I'm sorry I dragged you into this."

"Did you have a suspicion that Chad was behind Emma's disappearance?" I was feeling slightly annoyed with Laura and Ellie that they'd kept all this information from me.

"I tried not to think about it. I wondered if it might be the case, but it didn't seem possible. Chad hasn't seen Emma since she was a baby. How would he recognize her? It didn't make sense." Laura trailed off. I felt like she had more to say, but if she did, she stopped herself.

"Do you know where he lives?" I asked.

Laura shook her head.

I thought for a moment, putting pieces together. "How would he know I was looking for Emma?"

Ellie spoke up now. "I expect he had the school under surveillance. Maybe he saw you there."

That seemed a stretch, but I left it for a moment, remembering the news I had. "Do you know that Emma has a phone?"

Laura didn't look up. "No, she doesn't. Remember? I told you that the other day. She's not allowed."

"She got a refurbished one from a teacher."

Her head snapped up. "What?"

"Mr. Williams, her math teacher."

"She didn't tell me. He gave it to her?"

"She bought it from him, apparently."

I could see anger building inside her. She sat up straighter. "He didn't ask me if that was okay." She thought for a moment. "Maybe he has her. Who gives a kid a phone? That's super creepy." Her eyes were flicking around the room while she processed this information.

"Did you not want Emma to have a phone so that she couldn't be found online?" I asked, but Laura didn't hear me.

She stood up and began pacing in front of the tall windows. "I'll kill that teacher. How dare he? I need to call the school. He needs to be fired."

It felt like Laura's worry was being alchemized into anger, giving her something to focus on other than her own fear. She fumed and paced, raising her voice and railing against Mike Williams' interference. Ellie waited patiently, sitting on one arm of the couch. I waited as well, though less patiently. After several minutes, Laura's pacing began to slow and the slightly crazed look began to leave her eyes.

When I felt she'd be able to focus, I asked my question again. "Was the reason you didn't want Emma to have a phone that without one, she wouldn't have an online presence?"

She heard me this time and nodded, coming to a standstill. "The women from the underground support group recommend not doing anything online, even with our new names. I don't have any social media accounts. I have email through work, but that's it. We've never had a computer, not that we could afford one. And until now, it hasn't been an issue with Emma. She's always been more interested in reading, learning, and drawing than in online stuff. I thought that was still the case." She chewed a fingernail. "Do you think this Mr. Willams was grooming her?"

"I'm not positive, but I don't think so. He seems like a genuinely good guy who was trying to help. He believes she was feeling pressure from her friends at school because she was the only kid without a phone."

I thought of one other thing that I needed to check with her. "Did you tell the school Emma was sick and that was why she missed school last week?"

Laura nodded. "I didn't want to get the cops involved, so I told the school she had the flu."

Ellie spoke again, bringing Laura back down to earth. "Even if it was inappropriate for the teacher to sell her the phone, he's not the one who kidnapped Emma."

Laura deflated, looking from Ellie to me. "You're right. With what happened to Freddie, now we know for sure it's Chad that has her."

I suspected that the possibility that Emma's math teacher was somehow tied up in her disappearance had seemed like a welcome distraction from the specter of Chad's involvement. Now that Laura had recovered from her outburst about Mr. Williams, we were back to the grim reality of what to do next.

ONE OF MY favorite features of my old house, in addition to the kitchen nook, was the old clawfoot tub in the upstairs bathroom. It was deep and wide and the perfect length for me. But the best thing about it was that when I leaned my head back while lying in it, it was comfortable for my neck. Not an easy thing to find in a bathtub.

I sank into it now, the scented bubbles that I'd put in rising up along my legs and torso as I slid under the water with a small groan of relief. I had candles going and there was a glass of red wine on the small table beside the tub, even though it was barely noon.

Laura, Ellie, and I had sat in Laura's apartment for a couple more hours discussing where to go from there. There was no general consensus. I thought we should go to the police. Ellie seemed to be on the fence about that, and Laura was determined, more than ever, not to. Now that she knew Emma was alive and that there was some hope that she was being treated properly—in other words, she hadn't been kidnapped by a stranger—her relief was palpable. But it was mixed with fear and dread, and I could see her anxiety rising once she got over the initial shock and relief of knowing that Emma was alive.

Laura was convinced that Chad would have police officers in his pocket, and, as she knew more about that world than I did, I decided to take her at her word, even if privately I felt she was being slightly paranoid. But I knew nothing about the world of drug runners and pimps that Chad apparently belonged to. Laura had described Chad as being a bad guy in Kelowna, someone all the other bad guys were afraid of. She'd painted him as ruthless and entirely unfazed by the death and destruction that he wrought in people's lives.

"But his charm is legendary," she'd told us. "If you met him on the street, you wouldn't have any idea who he was. You'd just think he was an average banker or teacher. He can turn on the charm, and it throws all his other characteristics into the shadows." Quite a poetic description, I thought.

Eventually we were all worn out, and I knew personally that I needed some time to think about what to do next. Ellie had brought me home after we had promised Laura that we would be in touch first thing the next day.

I was hoping that by having some calm, quiet time to

myself, the answer about what to do next would become clear. The thought of Emma being held captive, essentially, by a man who was her father but whom she had never met and had no memory of was frightening. I wondered what she was going through. No doubt the picture that Laura had painted Emma of her father was a sharp contrast to whatever she was experiencing now.

I thought about going to Mack without telling Laura. I trusted him implicitly, and I knew with 100 percent certainty that he was not a dirty cop. But he was the only police officer I could say that about. I had no idea who he knew in the department nor who he might ask for help or get involved in the case if I mentioned it to him. And if what Laura said was true, by talking to Mack I could put Emma in considerable danger.

The more I pondered things, the more I realized that I was entirely out of my depth, caught between a rock and a hard place. I took a sip of wine and set it back down on the table, and felt my chest tighten. I started to cry.

No doubt the tears were left over from the shock of the home invasion the night before. I let them flow and wiped my face occasionally with a washcloth. When I was done, I was left with the cleansing feeling that comes with the release of pent-up fear and anger. There really was no other feeling like it. I felt empty and soothed at the same time. But I still didn't have any answers about what to do about Emma. I closed my eyes and let myself sink deeper into the bathwater.

"Bummer about the glass bird."

I opened my eyes and saw Blythe sitting on the edge of the tub near my feet.

"Where were you when I was being attacked earlier?" Even to my own ears my tone sounded bitter.

She shrugged. "I don't understand it, but somehow it's not me that decides when I show up." She was wearing a dress that I recognized as one of her favorites.

"And how come you're clothed? Shouldn't you be in angelic robes or something?"

She looked down at herself and then back up at me. "I think what I'm wearing has more to do with you than with me."

I supposed that made sense.

"You need a bad guy," Blythe said.

I scrunched my face up at her, confused. "What?"

"You know that expression, 'It takes a thief to catch a thief'?"

I nodded.

"In this case, I think you need a bad guy to catch a bad guy. What do you know about the world of drug kingpins and motorcycle gangs or whatever?"

"Absolutely nothing," I said.

"Exactly. So if you're going to find Emma, you're going to need somebody who knows how that world works."

I leaned my head back on the edge of the tub for a moment, closed my eyes, and thought about that. Then I said, "How do I find that person?" I waited, but didn't hear an answer.

I cracked my eyes open, but Blythe was gone.

Chapter 17

After my bath I spent a few hours in my studio. Both those things helped to help me to feel grounded and more like myself once again.

While I painted, Blythe's phrase about 'a bad guy' kept running through my head, and my subconscious seemed to be chewing over her suggestion. I was working on the gray rocks beneath the tree I was painting when I had an idea about how to find such a person. It was a long shot, admittedly. My Rolodex wasn't exactly stacked with nefarious individuals. My friends tend to be other artists, bookish types, and entrepreneurs.

Sometime after 3 o'clock I got dressed to go out and see about finding a bad guy.

I walked east from my house to Main Street, turned left and immediately saw the person I was hoping to see. When I approached him, Christopher smiled. As ever, he was too thin for his frame, but his eyes were bright despite the steady drizzle.

I had known Christopher for several years, just from seeing him around the neighborhood. And then a few months ago we had grown closer due to an unusual set of circumstances. He had gotten pulled into what I would now describe as a cult, and when his friend Rory had alerted me to Christopher's disappearance, I'd spent a few weeks trying to find him. That event had brought us closer together. It was also the reason Ellie had asked me to help find Emma.

Christopher was a lovely young man with some mental health issues. For years he had slept rough in the park in our neighborhood, but now he had a small studio apartment in a social housing building down the hill. He was clean and sober, as well as being an artist. He was also a sweetheart who had been dealt a very difficult hand of cards in this lifetime. I often wished I could do more for him.

"Hey, Freddie," he said.

"Have you had lunch?" It was a stupid question. The only reason he was standing on this corner was to raise money to buy food. His welfare checks never stretched far enough after he paid the rent and utilities. He shook his head.

"Let me treat you."

He accepted and we went across the street to a place that serves all-day breakfast. I had my favorite eggs Benny, while Christopher ate his half-weight in pancakes and corned beef hash. I stayed quiet while we ate, simply letting him focus and enjoy his meal; toward the end I could see some color coming into his face. When he finished, he leaned back and patted his belly.

"That was awesome. Thank you."

"My pleasure."

Our waitress came over and poured Christopher a refill on his soda and took his plate away.

When she was gone, I said, "I have kind of an odd question for you."

He looked slightly surprised but took it in stride. "Shoot."

I gave him a brief overview of the situation so far, leaving out Laura's and Emma's names. I didn't think I could just come in out of nowhere and ask if he knew anyone nefarious.

I felt I needed to give him an explanation and some background for why I was asking. And at the end, I explained that I was looking for somebody who might live ever so slightly outside the law who in turn might know or know of a local bad guy named Chad Allen.

Christopher thought about this for a few moments. The waitress came back and set the bill on the table. When she had gone away, he shook his head and I felt the sting of disappointment.

"I don't," he said. "But you know who would?"

I was starting to shake my head and then I guessed what he was thinking.

"Rory," we said together.

RORY, last name unknown, was Christopher's close friend. He also had a long stretch of homelessness behind him and now lived in the same building as Christopher. Usually, when I saw one of them panhandling in our neighborhood, the other one could be found close by.

Where Christopher was quiet and polite and probably introverted, Rory was more boisterous and extroverted. He was always chatting somebody up on the street. He was known around the neighborhood for usually having two hats on his head. The bottom one was an old woolen beanie that had holes in it from use and age, and then on top of that he would place a grimy baseball hat. The reasoning was simple, according to Rory. The beanie kept him warm, and the baseball hat was what he used when he panhandled. He would hold the baseball cap out in front of himself with the dome down, and when anyone gave him change or a bill from their wallet it went into the baseball cap rather than into his hand.

There was an honesty and something trustworthy about Christopher. I never felt like he was on the make with me when he asked for change or for help buying groceries. This was not exactly the case with Rory, however. Anytime I had a conversation with him I always felt like he was gaming me, even if the conversation was completely innocuous. So it was no surprise, really, that he was who Christopher had thought of when I said I needed to find someone who lived slightly outside the law.

Christopher thought that he had seen Rory outside a liquor store a couple of blocks south of where we were, so after lunch we walked in that direction, and indeed, that's where he was. He smiled when he saw us, and bumped fists with Christopher when we joined him.

I had thought ahead and brought with me a to-go meal from the breakfast place; two egg sandwiches with ham and cheese on toasted English muffins. I handed the bag to Rory. He looked inside and his eyes lit up.

He placed the baseball cap on top of his beanie and wasted no time unwrapping the first sandwich and taking a big bite. He was reed thin, like Christopher, and always looked like he needed to bathe; this had seemed natural when he'd been living out of doors, but now that he had his own apartment it was a little surprising. His brown eyes were bright and intelligent, when he wasn't high, that is, and there was a faint hint of Newfoundland in his speech.

"Let's go sit down so you can enjoy your sandwiches," I said.

The three of us walked around the corner and sat on a low stone wall that bordered the alley behind the liquor store. The rain had stopped for the moment, making dining al fresco slightly more comfortable.

While Rory chewed, once more I told the story of Laura and Emma. I ended by saying that I was looking for a bad dude named Chad and that, consequently, I needed to speak to someone who might know Chad or know the circles he moved in.

Rory listened to my explanation but looked confused. Around a bite of sandwich, he said, "So you're looking for a drug dealer?"

"Not necessarily. I just… I'm trying to find out more about this Chad guy, but I don't know anyone who dabbles in crime or who hangs out with people like that."

"So you came to Christopher and me?" Rory wiped the corner of his mouth with the back of his hand. He looked offended.

"Not with the expectation that you would know Chad." I was backpedaling. "I'm grasping at straws and thought…"

Rory let out a weird chuckle and pushed my shoulder with two slightly greasy fingers. "I'm just messin' with ya. I knew right away who I could introduce you to. Come with me." He balled up the wax paper that had wrapped his second sandwich and stuffed it back into the brown paper bag, where it joined the wrapper from the first one. He'd inhaled them both in record time. Then he crumpled the bag and set it beside himself on the wall. He stood up, wiped his hands on his jeans and started to walk away. I followed, but not before picking up the paper bag and shoving it in my purse. Christopher saw me and raised an eyebrow.

"Don't be a litter bug," I said as we scurried down the alley after Rory.

Together the three of us walked south on Main Street, past the poodle-on-a-pole sculpture that had confounded the neighborhood when it had been put up a few years ago. It was literally a larger-than-life-sized white standard poodle sitting on top of a 20-foot-high pole. As an artist, I adore public art and sculpture, but even to me this installation was baffling.

Rory led us about three blocks past the poodle and then turned into a store that advertised itself as selling vinyl records. 'Hep Cat Vinyl' was painted on the glass of the sky-blue door.

The store was clean and bright, with walls painted a

cheery yellow. The wooden racks that held a cascading assort-
ment of records were painted turquoise, and there were two
or three floor-to-ceiling columns around the room that had
been painted a terra-cotta orange. Someone had an apprecia-
tion for color.

The store was empty when we walked in. I had always
questioned the business model of selling vinyl records. I knew
there was a huge nostalgic market for them, but I was also a
little dubious about how a business like that actually made a
profit.

A beaded curtain, circa 1969, hung in a doorway at the
back of the shop, and momentarily a small blond man
emerged through it. I could see immediately that he recognized Rory, and then his eyes flicked to Christopher and me.

"Rory, my man, what can I do you for this fine
afternoon?"

The man had a jovial face and sparkling eyes that were an
indistinct color, something between blue and brown. He had a
pronounced widow's peak, and his thin blond hair looked like
soft down. He was slender and petite, maybe 5' 6", and looked
as though he hadn't eaten a carb in living memory. He was
wearing a long-sleeved shirt, striped in blue and white, with a
dark vest over it, like the vest from a suit. And a red bowtie.

He and Rory performed a complicated fist-shaking and
bumping thing over the counter where the cash register was,
and then Rory introduced us.

"Anthony, this is my friend Christopher and our friend
Freddie."

Anthony nodded to us both. "Pleased to meet you. Can I
interest you in a vinyl record?" He pointed a finger at Christopher. "I'm a bit of a maestro when it comes to matching
people to music. I peg you as a…" He thought about it for a
few seconds and then said, "Red Hot Chili Peppers. No! Wait.
That's not quite right. Don't tell me." He held up a hand,

asking for our patience. After a few seconds he snapped his fingers and said, "U2."

"That's right," Christopher said. He sounded both surprised and delighted. It was like Anthony had done a magic trick.

Anthony's attention swiveled over to me. "You're going to be a little tougher, I can tell." He stroked his chin with his hand, and I wasn't sure if the gesture was habitual or if he was doing it for comic effect. We all stayed quiet while he thought, looking me over from head to toe. This felt a little uncomfortable, but given that he had announced his intention, it exactly didn't feel creepy. Finally he said, "I'm a little bit stumped, but I'm going to say… Norah Jones."

"Wow," I said. "You really are good at that."

He looked pleased with himself. He gave his vest a tug and looked pleased with himself.

"Now, what can I do for you folks? I've got a fine copy of 'Not Too Late' that just came in, like, three days ago," he told me.

I wasn't actually a Norah Jones fan. I had just agreed with him to make him happy and lull him into a sense of camaraderie. I guessed it was time to put my money where my mouth was. I didn't even own a record player, but I got him to lead me over and show me the album. And I let him talk to me about it for quite a while.

When he was done, I purchased the record; he put it into a paper bag and I tucked it under one arm. At that point I gave Rory a look and a little nod with my head. God bless him, he knew what I was indicating.

"Hey, Anthony, we also wanted to ask you a question," Rory said. "Freddie here is looking into the disappearance of a little girl."

To his credit, Anthony's face fell immediately. It didn't seem like an act, and I thought that with that kind of empathy we might get some help from him, whatever his nefarious connections.

Rory continued. "And she's looking for a guy you might know about. Chad Allen."

Anthony froze and his expression went from empathetic to deeply wary in a nanosecond. Rory, Christopher, and I waited, watching him. Finally he moved. Walking around the end of the counter, he went past us to the front door of the shop. We all turned, watching him, like three monkeys at a tennis match. There was a loud click as he locked the deadbolt on the front door. He flipped the 'Open' sign to 'Closed' and then turned and faced us.

"Who sent you?" he said.

Chapter 18

Anthony's demeanor had suddenly turned from jovial host to something like a rat trapped in a corner by a broom. His change in energy spooked Christopher and Rory, and they started apologizing and making lots of noise, shuffling around, making steadying motions with their hands, which only made Anthony more frightened. This was a man who had something to hide.

"No one sent us," Rory explained. "Freddie is just trying to help a friend of hers."

"You guys gotta leave." Anthony unlocked the door again and cracked it open, making ushering movements. "Out! I don't have anything to say."

I moved toward him, "Wait, Anthony, I'm just…"

"I'm going straight," he said, with a slight whine in his voice. "I've stopped dealing and I'm making a go of it with this shop. My parole is over in six months, and I'm not going to do anything to jeopardize that. I need you to leave."

Rory and Christopher began moving toward Anthony, talking over each other. I gave them both a sharp look to shush them, and they dutifully shushed. Then I turned to Anthony and willed myself to be as still and calm as possible.

Years ago I took an Equus class as part of my search for healing after Blythe died. The training involved getting into a round pen with a horse and trying to bond with it, using just your energy. It's harder than it sounds. Horses, though they are large, are prey animals, and as a result are highly attuned to their environment and to the energy of those around them.

One of the lessons we learned that weekend that has stuck with me ever since is that the lead mare in any heard of horses is not the strongest. She's not the fastest. And she's not the one with the quickest temper. She's the *calmest*. That lesson popped into my head now as Anthony's wide eyes and rigid stance spoke volumes about how afraid he was at the mention of Chad's name.

I tried to exude my lead mare energy.

I said to Anthony, "We're not here to cause you trouble. I'm just looking for information about a little girl who's missing."

Anthony began to object, saying he didn't know anything about any little girl, and I realized that I'd phrased things incorrectly.

I stayed calm. "I don't think you had anything to do with that, Anthony. I'm looking for information about who might have taken her, and that's why we're interested in Chad Allen." I stopped talking and just stood in the middle of the store, looking at Anthony with the expectation of an answer but without aggression. To my right, Rory started to move and speak again. I made a small motion with one of my hands, and, thankfully, he caught the message and closed his mouth.

The four of us stood quietly, waiting, while Anthony made his decision. The seconds ticked by. I concentrated on breathing slowly though my nose. Then, finally, he closed the door again with a quiet click and reapplied the deadbolt. Without saying a word, he walked through the store, past me and my two amigos, and back toward the beaded curtain.

When he got there and was about to push his way past the beads, he made a beckoning motion with his hand.

I didn't need asking twice. We followed him.

He led us into a storeroom that was a mishmash of metal shelving units, stacked boxes, and a tiny kitchen counter with a kettle, toaster, sink, and microwave. The shelving units held boxes of what I assumed were more vinyl records, and also industrial-sized packages of toilet paper, paper towels, and cleaning agents. Commingled with the scents of dust and burrito, the room smelled faintly of pot. Anthony had better hope his parole officer never came back here, I thought.

Our host positioned himself near one of the metal racks and then turned and looked at us. "I'll give you two minutes and then you need to leave. I'm risking a lot just having this conversation."

Rory started to speak again, and I felt bad but I spoke over him. "Anthony, maybe you can just tell us anything you know about Chad. We're starting from scratch, and I'm simply trying to find his daughter. We think he may have kidnapped her from her mother."

Anthony let out a big breath, crossed his arms over his chest, and stared at me belligerently. "If he's got her, you'll never find her."

"Fair enough. But maybe you could just tell us what you know." He seemed unmoved, so I decided to try a little flattery. "You're obviously the guy to speak to, because Rory thought of you as soon as I asked the question. So clearly you're well connected."

My approach didn't seem to work at first, but then, after a few seconds, Anthony's face softened and he made a little adjusting movement with his shoulders and back.

"Here's what I know," he began. "Chad is a bad guy, and you don't want to mess with him. I had a friend who got into debt with Chad, and it did not end well. Let me say that."

I nodded, listening calmly while shivering internally.

"He mostly works in the drug trade, of course. The hard stuff, too. Pills and heroin."

"Is he a junkie himself?" I asked, hopefully, thinking Chad would be easier to deal with if he was out of it half the time.

But Anthony shook his head. "Nope. Doesn't even drink. Nothing. His body is a temple, as they say." He rolled his eyes.

"What else? Anything else you can tell us will be helpful, Anthony," I said, keeping my voice calm and level. "I'm starting with nothing."

He thought for a moment. "Let's see. I've heard he mostly lives in a penthouse in a new building in Yaletown that he bought." This confirmed what Laura had suspected, and I let Anthony keep talking. "I think he also has a place up at Whistler, but I don't think he spends too much time up there. He runs his operation with a style that is like micromanaging on speed. Nothing moves that he doesn't know about it." He stopped, and I could see him thinking, so I continued to keep my mouth shut. After a moment he said, "He owns a couple of legitimate businesses around town that he washes money through. A dry cleaner on West Broadway, and—what do you call it? A garage for where you get your car fixed."

"Where is that one?" I had pulled out the notepad from my purse and was jotting these things down.

"It's between Cambie and Main on Eighth or Seventh. You know, that …sort of a light industrial area over there. There's a bunch of ICBC repair shops. Near where the Canadian Tire is."

I nodded, picturing the neighborhood that he was describing.

"What else? Any other businesses or places where we might find him? Any close associates or friends that he has? Any weird hobbies?" I didn't even really know what questions to ask; I was just stabbing in the dark. But now that we had

Anthony talking, I didn't want him to stop. Who knew where the valuable information was? I would just have to sift through it.

"He has a couple of top lieutenants, but he's not an absentee boss, that's for sure. Like I said, anything that moves, he knows about it. I suppose he knows the other crime bosses in town, but I don't think he has anyone he's particularly close to. But what the hell do I know? I'm not his best friend. I just know what I hear on the street."

Anthony's mention of the word 'lieutenant' got me thinking. "Is one of his lieutenants a slender guy who wears expensive suits?"

Anthony's mouth curled into a bitter smile. "Oh, yeah. That's Ray Murphy. He and Chad have been together for years. He mostly does Chad's muscle work. Not personally, of course. He has a couple of meatheads that he drags around with him. But when Chad needs somebody roughed up, Ray's the guy he sends. He's a sociopath. He loves hurting people. You should hear some of the stories I've heard from the women he's dated."

I was afraid Anthony was going to tell us some of those stories, so I tried to divert his attention. "Any other businesses that you know of that he runs?"

We went back and forth like this for another five or ten minutes, but there was wasn't really anything more that Anthony could add to what he had already said. He didn't know the address of the building where Chad lived, but he described it and give me one of the cross streets, so I figured I'd be able to find it.

We were just about to wind up when there was a tapping at the front door of the store. All four of us jumped. Anthony looked through the beaded curtain and said, "I gotta go. That's a customer. You guys can leave through the back."

The tapping came again, more insistent. Anthony hurried

over to a metal door at the back of the shop and unlocked it. He opened it and held it for us. As we passed through, I thanked him for his help.

"You can thank me by never coming back here again." He closed the door firmly behind us.

Chapter 19

How does one go about surveilling somebody? I had no idea. When I got home late Sunday afternoon, after walking back to my street with Christopher and Rory, I did some googling, trying to gather any tips I could. Unfortunately, I was on my own and I learned that was going to be a huge disadvantage. Eventually, I closed my laptop with a grunt and headed upstairs to bed.

I slept badly. I went down to the main floor in the middle of the night on two separate occasions to check that the front and back doors were both locked and the windows were secure. I had thought of asking Ellie if I could sleep on her couch again, but decided if I was going to get used to being comfortable in my home again, I might as well start immediately.

In the morning, showered and fed, I filled my reusable water bottle, grabbed my travel coffee mug, and headed out to Loretta Jetta to see what I could accomplish that day. I dressed in layers, thinking I would be sitting in the car for long periods of time, which turned out to be true. I brought a couple of different scarves, and even an old fleece blanket to put over my legs. It was November, after all, and though Vancouver temperatures are milder than the rest of the country in the winter, it was still cold outside.

I took the Cambie Street bridge and followed Anthony's directions into Yaletown. He had described Chad's building as a glass and concrete residential tower with commercial suites on the ground floor. What made it distinctive were the two fiberglass Orca sculptures out front; one painted bright pinks, oranges, and blues, and the other covered with small dancing human figures and cityscapes. The sculptures were part of a fundraising effort by a local charity and had been popping up all over the city. Anthony had said he thought the building was on Pacific Boulevard, and he was right.

I sailed past the building and then did two loops around the block, getting a sense of where people would enter and exit. Pacific is a busy, four-lane thoroughfare, which was much better for me than if the building had been on a quiet side street. Hopefully my stealth activity would be lost in the constant flow of cars, trucks, motorcycles, bicycles, and buses.

I needed the perfect parking spot on the opposite side of the street from which to watch the front door and the alley exit. As with any large city, parking is always the biggest headache. I circled the block for nearly 45 minutes until someone pulled out of a spot that looked like it would work for me. It was a little farther away than I wanted, but I thought that was better than being too close to the building. I had brought an old pair of binoculars that my dad had given me for my twelfth birthday in the hopes that I would take up birding with him. I never had, but I was appreciating the gift for the first time now.

The front doors of the building, and the retail spaces, faced Pacific. Access to the parking garage was on the side of the building in an alley, which was unfortunate. If Chad and/or his henchmen came out of the garage and turned right, I'd be able to see them. If they went the other way, toward the back of the building, I wouldn't.

For that entire day I was very cautious; I didn't get out of the car other than to feed the parking meter and grab a quick lunch and take a pee break. I assumed that, like most commercial structures, the building had security cameras, so I wanted to minimize my exposure to those. And if Chad owned the building, like Anthony thought, then I figured his crew would recognize me if they looked closely at the footage. I was wearing a baseball cap and a big floppy scarf that covered my chin, but Gray Suit and his two thugs knew what I looked like. I had no idea if Chad himself did, but I wasn't taking any chances.

I SAT THERE ALL DAY. I was worried that if a parking control officer happened to notice that I'd been parked there for longer than the maximum two hours I'd have to move the car, but luckily that didn't happen. An officer did come by once around mid-afternoon, but just made a note that there was money in the meter and moved on.

There's no doubt about it: surveillance on your own is a loser's game. I tried to drink as little as possible, but still, the bladder can only handle so much. Around noon, my back teeth nearly floating, I went into an upscale grocery store around the corner to use their washroom, and bought some snacks and a chickpea salad for my lunch.

As the day wore on, I got to recognize the older residents, the ones who walked their dogs every few hours, trundling out of the front door of the building with little apartment dogs on long stringy leashes. One lady came out of the building with a dark gray, almost blue, mastiff that likely weighed far more than its owner. That dog was much more placid and mellow than the tiny dogs.

And of course, all that sitting around gave me plenty of time to ponder. How did somebody run a crime organization out of a penthouse in Yaletown anyway? Did Chad hold meetings in the loft? I was fairly certain he probably wouldn't keep his product there. He must have a warehouse somewhere for that sort of thing. Do you warehouse drugs? I really had absolutely no clue what I was doing or how the criminal underworld worked, for which I was very grateful. But a little more information about the inner workings of the industry might have been beneficial to me.

Vehicles went in and out of the alley all day, and that was when my binoculars came in handy. None of them were the black SUV with tinted windows that had driven away from my house on Saturday night. All the vehicles just looked like your average citizen sedans and small SUVs. One person rode in on a Vespa, wearing a giant pink helmet. That was the most interesting event of the day.

By 2 o'clock, my bum was sore and my fingers felt frozen even though I had stretchy dollar-store gloves on.

At 5:45, I woke myself up making a snorting noise and realized I'd fallen asleep. What a pro. I figured it was time to go home.

Chapter 20

A day and a half later, I was no further ahead and felt like I was running out of options. I had even resorted to googling 'how to find a missing person'. It hadn't told me anything I didn't already know.

On Wednesday morning, before I did my next stint of surveillance, I took Ellie with me over to Laura's to give her what I felt would amount to an update without much information.

When Laura let us into her smoky apartment, I immediately noticed she'd lost weight. The place was messier than ever, now with clothes scattered on the living room floor. Ellie insisted on making Laura something to eat.

Laura shook her head and said, "I feel ill. How can I eat when Emma is out there in danger?"

Ellie leaned down from her great height and put both hands on Laura's shoulders. "Honey, if you don't stay strong for Emma, she won't have anyone to come home to. You have to take care of yourself."

Laura sighed mournfully. "I can't."

Ellie straightened her spine and looked at Laura, who had turned to stare out the sliding glass doors. She glanced at me with worry in her eyes and then picked the cigarette bowl up off the coffee table and took it with her into the kitchen, I assumed to throw out the butts. She bustled around in the kitchen. I heard water running, and figured she was starting to do the dishes that had been piled in the sink since we'd first started to come visiting. If Laura wasn't eating, she wasn't contributing to the dirty dishes, but she wasn't cleaning them up, either.

With Ellie busy, I decided now was as good a time as any to give Laura my non-update. We were sitting on the couch together, though her face was turned away, looking out the front windows.

"Laura," I began. "I don't have much to share, but I wanted to let you know I'm still searching."

I told her about the information I'd got about Chad's legitimate business and how my plan was to watch it and see if Chad appeared so I could follow him.

She listened, but without much enthusiasm. When I was done, she said, "He always had a few businesses that he owned. He called them investments, but they were really places to launder money."

This lined up with what Anthony had told us at the record store.

I didn't have anything to add, so I stayed quiet. So did Laura, who was still lost in her own thoughts.

On the coffee table in front of us there was a file folder that I hadn't seen before, open and spilling photographs out. The photographs were of a chubby baby with wispy hair and a big grin on her face. There was a scene taken outside, perhaps at a park. I could see green trees, blurry in the background. And there was a photo of the same child on someone's lap, but the adult wasn't in the frame.

For something to say, and to see if I could pull Laura out of her misery, I said, "Is this Emma?"

Laura glanced at the photos and touched one of them. "Yes."

"She was a gorgeous baby. She obviously takes after her mother." I smiled encouragingly.

Laura touched her fingertip to the top photograph and pulled it toward her, exposing a few more underneath it. There was an image with tiny Emma, held by two grownup hands and sitting in the saddle of what I assumed was a pony. The focus of the photograph was the child; the adults and the pony were mostly out of frame. Emma was screaming at the top of her lungs, her face contorted and scarlet in a way that only an unhappy infant's can be.

I chuckled softly and looked at Laura. "She wasn't the pony's biggest fan."

The tiniest flicker of awareness appeared on Laura's face. "Chad's parents thought it would be a good idea to bring a pony to her first birthday. I told them she was too young, but they insisted. She hated it, of course. The guy who brought the pony wore a huge cowboy hat and she was terrified of him, too. I think that was worse than the fear of the pony."

This was the most that Laura had said since we'd arrived. It was encouraging, though, and I tried to keep her talking for no other reason than that I could empathize with her. I still enjoy the bittersweet feeling of talking about Blythe. I love it when people ask about her, and I love it when I'm with my parents and a memory comes up and we share it. After Blythe died, all I wanted to do was talk about her, to tell people what a great person she had been and how unfair it was that she was gone, killed by a stupid tree. I wanted to tell her funny stories to others and see them laugh. Not that Emma was dead, of course, but I suspected that Laura might feel a similar sort of urge.

I asked, "Did she ever lose her fear of cowboy hats?"

A tiny smile appeared on Laura's face. "I'm not sure. You don't see many cowboy hats in Vancouver."

This was true.

Laura continued to pull the photographs forward one at a time. They were in a little stack in the file folder and she shared them with me one by one, explaining where each one was taken and how old Laura was at the time. They were mostly baby photographs; there were none where she was older than about a year. I noticed that any other people had been cropped out, except for Laura herself. Sometimes the photos were blurry, and it seemed to me like maybe they had been enlarged and then cropped.

It took me a moment, but I realized these must be photographs from the time when Laura was with Chad. I said as much to her and she nodded.

"I didn't want to put these in an album or anything because the memories from that time are just too awful. But I also didn't want to get rid of them. Emma might want them when she's a little older. So I just kept them in this file with her original birth certificate and stuff."

I could see some bureaucratic-looking paperwork at the bottom of the file folder when we had examined all the photographs. We came to a birth certificate that said Catherine Elizabeth Allen.

Tingles ran down the backs of my arms. I looked at Laura. "Did Emma know her original name?"

Laura shook her head, gazing at a photograph of Emma sitting on one of those baby swings in a park, the kind that are like a little bucket with two holes for the baby's legs to go through.

"No," she said. "I am going to tell her eventually, but I think she's too young right now."

The tingles on my arms continued and spread to my back. I sat very still, listening to Ellie bustling about in the kitchen. I could hear the burbling sound of the coffee maker and the click of her heels on the linoleum, in addition to the sounds of dishes being washed in the sink. Laura was lost in thought again beside me. I thought about what I knew about thirteen-year-old girls. There was one thing I remembered vividly from being that age: I was a snooper. At Christmastime, our mother had had to hide the presents for Blythe and me at a friend's house because she knew if she left them anywhere in our house, we would find them.

"Where did you keep this file?" I said to Laura.

"In my dresser." She looked across the room to a three-drawer dresser that stood against the far wall, beside the TV stand. "At the back of a drawer, underneath underwear and stuff."

I looked around the apartment for a computer and then remembered there wasn't one, so I reached into my purse and pulled out my phone. I went to the Instagram app and tapped my thumb on the search box. I entered in 'Catherine Allen' and hit search. I came up with a number of people and scrolled through them, holding the screen close to my face so I could see the profile images. None of them looked like a thirteen-year-old girl.

Beside me, Laura had slouched herself back into the recesses of the couch and was picking at her cuticles.

Ellie appeared with a mug of coffee and what looked like it might be a tuna and lettuce sandwich on white bread. She set both down in front of Laura and in a schoolteacher voice said, "We're not leaving until you eat that sandwich."

Laura looked up at her defiantly, but after a few moments of a staring contest, she heaved herself forward again, picked up half the sandwich, and took a bite, chewing and staring belligerently at Ellie.

Ellie give a sharp nod. "Good girl." She turned and went back to the kitchen.

I was still scrolling through Instagram profiles. I tried variations of the name 'Catherine Elizabeth' without luck. Finally, I dropped the phone to my lap and stared out the windows; a memory was tickling the back of my mind. I remembered the poster in Emma's room of *My Fair Lady*. I brought up the search box again and typed in 'Eliza Allen.'

Instantly, there she was. The tiny, circular profile photo of Emma Reid. Her handle was Eliza_Allen.

～

I DEBATED for a hot second not telling Laura about what I'd found, but that decision was taken out of my hands. Literally. I heard a little gasp beside me and realized she was looking over at my phone.

"Is that Emma?" she said.

With lightning speed she set the tuna sandwich down and snatched the phone out of my hand, her eyes glued to the screen. "It is."

She looked up at me and then back at the phone. "It's Emma, isn't it?" A little sob escaped her, and I could see her shoulders vibrating gently with emotion.

"It looks like she set up a social media account using her original name, with a nod to her favorite musical," I said.

"That little cow," Laura said, but it was spoken with a tremendous amount of affection. "She must've found the folder." Absentmindedly, she touched her coffee table while she said it, indicating the folder that we'd been looking at. Then she looked up at me. "What does this mean? You said she had a phone, right? That's how she must've created this account."

I nodded, agreeing. "I assume so. Look through her followers and the people she's following and see if you recognize anybody."

Ellie must have overheard us. She came out of the kitchen and stood on the far side of Laura, between the end of the couch and the sliding glass door. Her hands were wet and had blobs of dish soap attached to them. She held them up with her elbows slightly bent, like a surgeon going into an operating theater.

Laura touched her finger to Emma's followers line and up popped a list of people. She scrolled down the screen quickly and then back up to the top again, and then began going through the list more slowly.

"It looks like these are mostly kids at school," she finally said.

"Have a look at who she's following."

Laura hit the back button and then did as I requested, scrolling slowly again.

"This is mostly celebrities, I think. And those friends from school."

I wasn't sure where this information was going to get us. I had guessed that one of the reasons for Emma to have a phone was so that she could have a social media account. From what I understood from my friend Sean Wong's extended family, teenagers spend an inordinate amount of time chatting with their friends and sharing videos on social media.

Beside me, Laura let out a little gasp. She dropped her hand, still clutching the phone, to her knee and stared into the middle distance for a second.

"What?" Ellie and I both said simultaneously.

Laura didn't answer. She sat frozen for another few seconds and then looked at the phone again. Her head craned forward until her nose was almost touching the screen. And then, under her breath, she said, "That's Chad's sister."

We were all silent for a few heartbeats.

"That's how Chad found her," Ellie said.

Chapter 21

I dug around in my purse and found my notebook and a pen. I got Laura to go back through both the followers and following lists and wrote down every name. Then, more importantly, I got her to tell me what each person's association with Emma was. Most were friends from school. One or two Laura didn't know, but when we drilled down into their accounts, it looked like they were students at the school as well. Justin from the pot-growing operation was there.

When we were finished, Laura went back to Emma's main profile page and looked through her posts. I could see selfies of Emma with Olivia and other girls. Poses that involved a lot of tongues sticking out and either goofy faces or Zoolander expressions.

Eventually Laura handed the phone back to me. I could see her thinking. I stayed quiet and let her collect her thoughts.

Finally she said, "So somehow she found this folder with her birth certificate. And she made the Instagram account using her birth name. And then she found Chad's sister. I don't know why she did that." She looked from Ellie to me and then back again, searching for answers.

I didn't entirely understand what had happened either, but I could make some guesses. "Remember what being a kid is like?" I said. "The world is mysterious and confusing. Adults have secrets and yet they think we don't notice. And that only makes us more curious about them. I wonder if Emma knew more about your life in Kelowna with Chad than she let on."

Laura shook her head, but it was without conviction.

I continued. "She might have overhead a conversation of yours at some point. She might not even have understood what she was hearing at the time. But later, she might have realized there were pieces of the puzzle—pieces of her—that she was missing."

Laura stood up and began to walk in a slow circle around the room, chewing her cuticles. "But how did she find Chad's sister specifically? Allen is a pretty common last name."

"She's a smart girl, honey," Ellie said. "And like Freddie said, she seems to have put some pieces together."

"That's how Chad found us." Laura was repeating what Ellie had said moments ago, coming to grips with what had happened. "Emma followed his sister, and someone must have noticed. But she doesn't look anything like she did as a baby," she said, exasperated, trying to disprove what had happened. In her mind, perhaps, if she could find the weak link in the string of events that had led to Emma being taken by her father, maybe this wouldn't be real. She was trying to wind back time. It wasn't going to work.

Ellie sat down on the arm of the couch. "However it happened, honey, I think this is good news. It gives us more cause to believe that Chad has Emma. Knowing that will only help us find her."

I agreed with Ellie, but I wasn't sure Laura heard what she'd said. It would likely take her some time to come to grips with what we'd discovered.

Ellie sat with Laura in the living room while I finished washing the dishes and thought about my next move. I did feel a slight sense of relief that I was probably on the right track in my pursuit of the infamous Chad. Until the discovery of the Instagram account, a significant portion of myself had still been questioning the validity of our assumption that Chad was involved, despite the three violent visitors I'd had on Saturday night.

Now, though, the dots were lining up closer together. It made sense that Chad had found Emma given that she did, in fact, have an online presence. I imagined that a man with power like he seemed to have would find it easy to employ some sort of web hacker-genius to trace Emma's school or home address.

I felt a renewed sense of purpose. It was time to get back on the job.

Chapter 22

Vancouver's city hall is an Art Deco building set on the crest of a hill at the intersection of Cambie and West 12th Avenue. Its north-facing facade has a view of False Creek, the downtown area, and beyond that, the North Shore Mountains. I approached it from the south, crossing 12th Avenue and keeping the building on my left, and went downhill, along Yukon Street, knowing I'd be back in a few hours.

After days of sitting in my car, my back and bum were sore and I was cranky. Monday in Yaletown had been a bust, as had Tuesday, which I'd spent outside Chad's dry-cleaning business at Broadway and Arbutus. Like at the Yaletown building, it had been difficult to find a parking space that was close enough to the business that I could see who was going in and out, but far enough away that they wouldn't notice me. There were bus stops on all four corners of the intersection, which prevented me from parking in a spot that gave me a clear view to the store. In the end, I chose a spot in the tiny parking lot of a paint and wallpaper store down the block and across the street. I got about two hours of observation in before a store employee in a navy-blue apron came out and asked me to leave if I wasn't a customer of the store. I gave up and went home, feeling discouraged.

The day after that, after Ellie and I had visited Laura, I'd sat in a different and better parking spot, this time near the auto repair shop that Chad reportedly owned. This was the most fruitful day of the week by far. I'd had a clear view of the comings and goings at the shop all day from a vantage point far enough down the block that I didn't think I'd been spotted. The day was long, however, and no one matching Chad's description had appeared. When the shop had closed at 5 PM, I'd headed home, wondering what the hell I was playing at.

But in the middle of the night, I had two ideas. I love it when my brain problem-solves while I'm asleep. It often does this when I'm having trouble with a painting, so it was encouraging to see it worked in other areas of life as well. I woke early and, given that I'd had more than enough time in my car that week, I decided to walk to do the two things I had planned that day, thanks to my brain.

The morning was cool and crisp, the temperature hovering a few degrees above zero, but I enjoyed walking in the rare sunshine. I was dressed for action; dark jeans, running shoes, a mid-thigh raincoat over a well-worn hoodie, gloves, a dark blue Vancouver Mounties baseball cap on my head, and my hair tied in a loose ponytail, low on my neck. The camera and telephoto lens that I use to capture images for painting were in a small backpack on my back.

My first stop was going to be the auto shop. Because I was on foot, I wanted to be extra cautious about not being seen around the building, so when I got north of Broadway, I skirted around the auto shop's block, giving it a wide berth. It was just after 8 AM and I wanted to be in position well before the shop's employees arrived.

The day before, I'd noticed a one-story building opposite but down the block from Chad's business that appeared to be unoccupied. I came at the building from the east and took a closer look. All the windows had plastic Venetian blinds on the inside, all of them turned into the closed position. But some of the blind slats were broken or bent, and I was able to peer through. I couldn't see much of the interior, but what I could see was empty except for two industrial sewing machines and two bolts of fabric on a table that was pushed against a wall. The room was unlit and looked dusty and abandoned.

Perfect.

The reason I was keen on this particular building was that it had a recessed entryway, which I was hoping would be a perfect vantage point for me to take photographs from. Not only that, the entryway had two ornamental evergreen trees in large terracotta pots on either side of it, as you approached from the sidewalk. The building had clearly been abandoned for a while, and the trees were now less ornamental and more orna-ugly. They had grown far too large for the pots they were in and looked unhealthy and uncomfortable, like two plump women stuffed into spandex pants. But they were ideal for me because they provided some cover for what I hoped would be a covert photo session.

I got into position, knowing that now it was a waiting game. If yesterday was any indication, the two employees would arrive at around 9 AM, 45 minutes after I got into position. I shrugged my backpack off my shoulders and got my camera ready. I stuffed my gloves into a pocket and took a few test shots, checking them in the camera's viewing window.

Today was day nine since Emma had last been seen. And I was starting to lose faith that there was anything I could do to help Laura find her. I was messing around in a field where I didn't belong, and my discomfort with keeping the police out of the situation was growing every day. Other than the discovery of Emma's Instagram account, the week had been a total loss so far in terms of making any progress, and as I stood in the cool morning, watching my breath clouds in the air in front of me, I wondered if and when I would go against

Laura's wishes and talk to Mack. I empathized with her reasons for not wanting to involve the police, but at the same time I was starting to feel it was irresponsible of me not to do so. Now that we were fairly certain Emma was with Chad, I supposed there was less likelihood she was in grave danger, but still...

I wondered how long Laura had suspected Chad was involved. In hindsight, I was guessing now that she'd wondered about that all along. Her reluctance to go to the police might have more to do with the cops who might be in Chad's pocket than with her previous experiences with them. Her suspicion of Chad could even have been unconscious, something her conscious mind refused to acknowledge but that nevertheless had an effect on her choices and behavior.

But...what did I know? I wasn't a psychologist. I was just an artist with cold seeping through the bottoms of her shoes. I shook my head and tried to think of other things. Running around in mental circles was not helping me.

At five to nine I started checking my watch every thirty seconds, and the butterflies in my stomach revved up. They were sensitive little buggers.

Right at nine, a car I recognized from the day before pulled up and parked at the far side of the auto shop's drive-way. A man got out and went to the human-sized door on the opposite side of the building, unlocked it, and went inside. Almost immediately, the oversized rolling door that almost filled the shopfront began to slide upward, revealing the dark innards of the business. I was grateful for that moment, as the man was facing me for the first time. I got several good shots of him, zooming in on his face. He seemed to be in his thirties, with medium-dark hair that flowed over his ears and collar, a clean-shaven face, and a slightly sour expression. He was nondescript in every way. Average height. Average build. Jeans and a navy-blue, bomber-style jacket that had 'Vancouver Canucks' emblazoned the front, green and white stripes down the sleeves, and the club's logo on the back.

Mr. Canuck turned and disappeared into the bowels of the shop, but I didn't have to wait long for another burst of activity. As had happened yesterday, I heard the second man coming before I saw him. He appeared seconds later on a crotch-rocket motorcycle, pulling in immediately behind the first guy's car. The bike was entirely black, no color anywhere. I suspected this guy thought he was Batman because he too was entirely clad in black. Black jeans. Black motorcycle boots. Black Kevlar jacket. Black gloves. And a black helmet with a visor tinted in, you guessed it, black. He turned the bike off, dismounted, and went into the shop through the now wide-open garage door, pulling the helmet off as he did. I got several shots of him but none that showed his face.

Despite the risk of being spotted, I decided to stay for a while to see if I could get a better shot. I stamped my feet lightly, trying to generate some heat. A few moments later, another vehicle arrived, parking on an angle in the shop's driveway. A man in a suit got out and went inside. A few minutes later, a taxi pulled up and he came out of the building, got into it, and left. As the taxi was pulling out, a smallish SUV pulled into a metered parking spot near the shopfront. An older man got out of the car and went into the shop. He was stout, but not fat, had salt-and-pepper hair cut close to his head, and walked with a slight limp. Fifteen minutes later yet another vehicle pulled up, this time driven by a woman in jeans and a bulky sweater. She went through the same routine of going into the shop, but when she came out, she didn't take a taxi; instead, she walked west toward Cambie. The older man had not reappeared. I took photographs of all these people, who I assumed were customers, dropping their cars off to be fixed. Then I caught a break when Batman came out and moved one of the cars from the driveway into the shop.

With his helmet and jacket off, he turned out to be a young Asian man.

After that, the activity stopped. I stood in my spot, hoping I was concealed, and waited for another hour and a half, but nothing else happened. By that time, I was starting to get restless, not to mention hungry. I hadn't felt like eating before I'd left the house this morning. There was a café up the hill near City Hall that made the best croissants. I started to fantasize about having one with a very fluffy latte. I made myself wait until 11 AM, and when nothing else had happened, I slid out from behind the overgrown potted tree and walked east, away from the shop, adopting an air of nonchalance and trying to be as invisible as possible.

AN HOUR LATER, fed and watered, I approached City Hall from the north, walking up the wide stone steps past the statue of a bewigged Captain George Vancouver to the tall doors that led into the main entry. Signs in the foyer directed me down one floor to the property department.

Inside, the building was cool and dark and had lost much of its charm, or at least I thought so. Bureaucratic offices always made me feel like my soul was being sucked out of my body through the soles of my feet. Other than that, my visit was relatively painless. I found the office I needed, took a number, and waited. Within 20 minutes of my number being called, I had the information I had come for.

Two days before, when I'd given up on trying to keep an eye on the dry-cleaning business, I had recalled that there was a reverse directory service available at City Hall. If you have the address of a building, you can look up the name and phone number of the person who owns the property. At City Hall, I had the addresses in hand of the two businesses Anthony had said Chad owned, plus the building in Yaletown.

The ownership that came back for all three addresses was a company name, Claremont Holdings, and the address was the same for each as well. It was the address of the Yaletown building.

On one hand, this was good information. It proved that the same person owned all three buildings. It also showed me that it was likely that the Yaletown building was Chad's headquarters. On the other hand, there wasn't a person named as the owner at those addresses, just the company name. Which meant that I could be on the wrong track entirely. So it was a case of good news and bad news.

After that I walked home, used the bathroom, got into Loretta Jetta, and was at Laura's building just after 3 o'clock for my second visit in two days.

She buzzed me in, and I climbed the stairs once more to the cigarette smell–infused apartment.

Laura's eyes were bright with expectation when she opened the door for me.

"Have you found anything?"

"Not really. But I want to show you some photographs and see if you recognize any of the people in them."

She let go of the door and walked inside. I closed it behind me and followed. She settled into her spot on the couch out of habit. The apartment was no less messy than it had been the first couple of times I'd seen it, but I was becoming immune to the clutter, as one does. I moved several tabloid magazines off the seat beside Laura and sat down. The camera strap was across my torso, opposite to my purse. I took it off and brought the photographs up in the small screen at the back of the camera. Laura lit a cigarette.

"Do you recognize any of these people?"

The first were the two employees of the dry-cleaning business, a middle-aged-looking Asian couple. I clicked through the photographs I had taken of them. They weren't very clear, given that my vantage point had not been great. Laura took a deep drag of her cigarette and shook her head. Then I came to the photographs from the mechanic shop from that morning. I clicked over to the first one of Mr. Canuck and she looked at it. She began to shake her head but then leaned in closer, squinting her eyes at the small screen.

"I think that might be Chad's friend Lawrence. I haven't seen him in years, of course, but it kinda looks like him."

"Do you know anything about Lawrence? Do you know his last name?"

Laura thought for a moment, flicking her cigarette filter absently with her thumb. "Randall?" she said. "Roberts? Something like that. I think it started with an R."

"Anything else?"

Laura shook her head again. "It's been over ten years, Freddie. I barely knew the guy at the time. He was just one of the jerks that hung around Chad, delivering drugs for him and doing other odd jobs like that."

"OK. What about this guy?" I clicked through to the next photograph, of Batman arriving on his bike. Laura peered at the screen again but shook her head. I clicked through the photographs of the customers, trying to find the shot of Batman without his helmet on. As I scrolled through, passing the shots of the customers, Laura took another drag of the cigarette and then tapped some ash into the bowl on the table. She glanced at the screen in my hands and stiffened.

"Wait. Go back."

I scrolled back to a shot of the woman who had dropped off her car.

"No," Laura shook her head. "Go back again."

I clicked the camera's back button and came to the shot of the older man with the limp. I remembered at that moment that I hadn't seen him come out of the shop.

Laura leaned forward toward the camera screen, her whole body attentive. She was silent.

I waited until I couldn't stand it any longer. "Do you know that man?"

She sat up straighter on the couch and pulled on her cigarette once more, and then made a small nodding motion with her head. Her eyes had become unfocused and she had mentally gone somewhere far away. "It's Chad's father."

———————————

Chapter 23

———————————

The story emerged slowly, and it required a lot of coaxing on my part. At first Laura refused to talk about it at all, writing off Chad's father as unimportant in the search for Emma. Eventually, though, I was able to convince her that every detail mattered. I made her a cup of coffee and even a tuna sandwich, following Ellie's lead from the day before.

Once she'd had a couple of bites of the sandwich and some sips of coffee, she seemed to recover slightly from the shock that she'd exhibited upon seeing the photograph.

I said gently, "Tell me about Chad's dad."

She was quiet for a long time; she had been badly traumatized—that much was easy to tell. And as the story emerged, it was clear to see why. The acorn hadn't fallen too far from the tree, it turned out. Chad was simply a younger version of his father, who was the original bully and abuser.

"They're best buddies," Laura said, taking a small bite of the tuna sandwich. She swallowed and continued. "They're almost identical."

"In the way they look?"

"That and the way they are as human beings." She grew quiet again, then set the sandwich down and lit up another cigarette. This conversation was obviously very difficult for her.

I told her I was proud of her for being willing to share the information with me. She made a scoffing noise.

"Was Chad's dad involved in the drug business too?" I asked.

Laura surprised me by shaking her head. "I don't think so. He had a car repair shop." She made a gesture toward the camera sitting in my lap. "And my sense was that it was a legitimate business. He was a bully and a liar and a braggart like Chad, but I don't think he went in for the illegal stuff. He was always really proud of his business. It was kind of out of character, but he used to go to businessmen's lunches and stuff like that. I think he was the first generation of his family to ever make any kind of decent money. He and his wife owned a house in a fancy part of town, and when Chad was growing up, he always had the latest video games and stuff. I think Mr. Allen was proud of what he'd achieved."

Her eyes were focused on something far away and I could see that the more she talked, the more she remembered. She continued on. "Actually, now I remember that just before Chad and I got married, he and his dad had a big fight. Chad's dad wanted him to work at the auto shop, but Chad was making five times as much money dealing drugs, so he refused. At first, he didn't tell his dad what he was doing, but when he was buying new cars and going to Vegas every couple of months, his dad caught on."

"And his dad didn't agree with what he was doing."

"He hated it. He was so angry when he first put two and two together. They had a huge fight in the backyard one day at a barbecue."

"Like a physical fight?"

"I didn't start out that way. It just started out as a conversation and then it got worse and, in the end, yeah, it started to get physical. Chad's dad took a swing at him. But there were so many other friends there that they were able to pull them apart."

"Did they keep fighting about it after that? Like, at other times?"

"I don't exactly remember. This was just before Emma was born. So I was actually trying to ignore the whole thing. And then after she was born, things got so bad between Chad and me that I wasn't really paying attention."

It seemed that whatever had happened, the two men had repaired their relationship if Chad's dad was now involved in the auto shop.

Laura seemed to pick up my line of thinking. She waved her hand at the camera again. "It makes sense, in a way, that Chad owns an auto mechanic shop. And that his dad is involved. That's not a stretch at all."

I thought for a moment, putting the picture together in my head, and then said, "What about Chad's mom?"

"What about her?"

"Is she someone who would be sympathetic to you and to Emma? In a grandmotherly kind of way?"

"Chad's mom is a piece of work too," Laura answered. "I saw her go after his dad with a tire iron once. I think she would have brained him if Chad hadn't caught her."

So this wasn't the Brady Bunch we were dealing with.

"I think Chad got most of his belligerence from Lydia, his mom. He got his physical attributes and the way he solves all problems with his fists from his dad. But from his mom he got his tendency to be a grade A jerk." Laura's expression had turned from traumatized to bitter.

"So she's not the grandmotherly type.?"

"Not even close. She's petty and vindictive and swans around like she's the Queen of Sheba. Her favorite thing was to buy whatever the latest designer outfit was. She always had those huge long nails that were just ridiculous." Laura held one hand an inch and a half in front of the other's fingertips, indicating the length of the nails. "She was really the boss of the household. Chad and his dad were big talkers and alpha dogs until she came around. And then they didn't fart without asking her permission first." Laura picked up her tuna sandwich and took another bite; I was pleased to see her eating. I was about to ask another question when she carried on by herself. "I went to her at first."

"To Chad's mom?"

Laura swallowed. "Yeah. When Chad started beating me, the first thing I did was go to his mom, expecting support. Knowing that he listened to her, I thought she could get him to stop. Do you know what she said?" She looked at me with incredulous eyes.

I shook my head.

"She said that if he was beating me, there must be a reason. And that I had to figure out how to fix the problem. She wasn't going to fix it for me." Laura's hands had started to shake. She reached for the cigarette pack but kept talking. "I asked her what would happen if he started to beat Emma. But she said that there was no way that he would ever do that." She made the snorting noise again. "She said that Emma would never deserve to be beaten like I did."

Good grief.

Chapter 24

I still had not laid eyes on Chad. Laura had described him when we'd first realized that it was likely him that had kidnapped Emma, but I hadn't seen anyone like that in or around the dry-cleaning business or the auto shop. It's possible he could have gone in and out of the Yaletown building without me seeing him, but I had no way of knowing.

I sat in my car, chewing the edge of my thumbnail, thinking about Chad's parents, and about Emma. It was Friday, the day after I'd spoken to Laura. Emma had been missing for ten days.

The night before, I'd decided that perhaps my best bet was to follow Chad's father and see where that led me. This was as close as I got to an idea for how to move forward.

Rain had started the night before and continued now, drumming on Loretta Jetta's roof and bouncing off the pavement beside the car. I had gone for a long walk that morning around Queen Elizabeth Park. I hadn't been getting any exercise lately, what with all the sitting in the car, and my mood was suffering for it. I had felt much fresher that morning after the long walk, even though I arrived back home soaked to the skin. A hot shower and a good breakfast and I was feeling slightly more optimistic about my plan.

I spent the day watching the mechanic shop again. Chad's father arrived, as he had the day before, at around 10 AM. Throughout the day, people dropped cars off and picked them up. And my anxiety grew.

I was parked so that when Chad's father, whose name Laura said was Flint, left I could follow him. And at 5:30 that's what I did. Mr. Allen, the original bully as Laura called him, came out of the building and went to where he'd parked his car. He always parked at the same meter and never seemed to feed it. I hadn't seen him receive a ticket, though, so I suppose he thought it was worth taking his chances.

He was facing east, so he pulled a U-turn and drove away. After I'd turned my ignition key three times, Loretta's engine fired and I followed at as much of a distance as I could manage. He turned left at the first corner and went up to Broadway and through the lights, and then turned right at City Hall onto 12th Avenue. By then a couple of cars had squeezed in between us, for which I was grateful. Just as when I'd followed Justin, I was straining my eyes and gripping the steering wheel tightly, trying to keep him in sight while also not raising his suspicions. We kept traveling west and crossed Cambie, then Oak and then Granville. The traffic got a little quieter west of Granville as we crossed the border into Kitsilano. When we got to Arbutus Street, the light turned yellow just as Mr. Allen went through the intersection. The two cars ahead of me stopped, of course. And I was trapped behind them.

I whispered, "Come on. Come on," under my breath the whole time the light was red. When it turned green, the cars took off. The road was one lane in each direction at this spot, so there was no way I could get around them. I carried on, searching the road ahead, hoping that Chad's dad had gotten stopped at a red light.

Driving and frantically scanning the road and trying not to drive into the back of the car ahead of me was not easy. I was swearing and sweating so much I nearly missed him. But just as I went through an intersection, I spotted him at a gas station, filling up.

I had to circle the block twice before I found a parking spot that allowed me to keep an eye on him. He returned the nozzle to the gas pump, paid with his card, then climbed into his car and pulled out onto the road again. We continued on the journey west, stopping and starting all the way along to Blenheim, where he turned left.

We went south about three blocks, with only one car between us, and then his car turned left onto 14th Avenue. I kept going and turned left at the next cross street, where I picked up speed and raced to the next corner. Left again, and then I slowed down dramatically and crawled along to the street where Mr. Allen had turned. I eased into the intersection and saw that he was parking his car about five doors down from the corner. There were no cars behind me on the quiet residential street, so I just sat there and watched as he got out of his car and walked into a house on the south side of the street.

My mind was racing, and I was wondering what to do next, and how to get a better look at the house. From the angle where I was idling, I made a note of the house's shape and color; I couldn't see the number from this distance. I thought I might park and walk down the street and then circle back through the alley behind the house.

I was just about to pull ahead to find a parking space when I noticed a giant black SUV parked opposite the house that Chad's father had gone into. My breath caught a little bit in my throat.

I glanced in my rearview mirror and there was still nobody behind me, so I threw Loretta into reverse and backed up until

I was beside the entrance to the alley that ran behind the houses.

There was another enormous black SUV parked illegally in the alley at about the place where Chad's father's house was.

The house was being guarded.

"I think I just found Emma," I said to Loretta.

Chapter 25

The next morning I surprised one of my neighbors by accosting him on his front walk. I knew that he usually walked his dog before 8 AM, even on the weekend. So when I saw him open the front door, I was ready. I burst out of my own front door and trotted across the street, waving and smiling.

The neighbor's name was Jim and he was in his early 60s. His wife had died two years previously, and one afternoon I took a casserole across the street to him. He'd invited me in and we spent a sad couple of hours talking about his wife's long battle with breast cancer. I had shared my story of Blythe's untimely death, and, in that strange way that grief works, it had created a connection between us. Before that, we'd just been neighbors who waved at one another on the street.

Since that visit we'd been friendlier, and whenever I was out for a walk and bumped into him, I would spend a few minutes chatting and petting his dog, whose name was Archie.

Jim was a lawyer who worked downtown and had done for some 40 years or so. He loved the law, and being a lawyer, he said, was the only thing he had ever wanted to do.

Archie was now the sole focus of Jim's affection and attention. He was a pampered dog but not spoiled. Jim had taken him to several obedience classes and Archie was very well behaved, more so than many of the other dogs in the neighborhood.

Because Jim worked long hours, Archie had a dog walker, a university student named Caroline who was partially paying for her education by walking dogs. Archie got picked up every day in the afternoon and went out with a pack of dogs of a similar size. I was so pleased when Jim told me this. There is nothing I hate more than learning about people who own dogs and leave them locked up at home for 12 hours a day.

"Good morning, Freddie," Jim said as I came up the pavement toward him. Archie began wagging his tail and wiggling his body. Is there anything better than the unconditional love from a dog?

Archie was a mixed-breed rescue. One day the summer before, when Jim and I had bumped into each other in a park, we'd sat and had a long chat on a bench while Archie ran around, chasing squirrels and sniffing every blade of grass and the other dogs' bums. We had debated about Archie's lineage and concluded that there was definitely some spaniel somewhere in there, but also possibly some German Shepherd. He was mostly black with a splotch of white on his chest and two white paws. He was definitely spaniel-shaped, but there was something about his head and nose specifically that reminded me of a Shepherd. We would never know, of course, and it didn't really matter. He was a friendly, smart, accommodating dog who loved everyone he met, man or beast. Except for squirrels.

On this Saturday morning, when Jim and I had concluded our preliminary greetings, asking each other about our well-being and then talking about the weather for a moment—our Canadian citizenship would have been revoked if we hadn't done that—I pitched my question to him.

"Hey, Jim, I wondered if I could borrow Archie today. Actually this morning."

He looked at me, a slightly puzzled expression on his face.

I told him the story that I had fabricated. I didn't think he would really want to hear that I was staking out a house where I thought a kidnapped girl was being held by her drug dealer father. "I'm going for a walk with my friend Marion today [total lie—I don't have a friend named Marion] and she has a dog. I thought it would be fun if I took Archie so we could all walk together."

Jim was better than most at sniffing out a lie, given his profession, but he seemed to accept what I had to say. I bent over and played with Archie's ears to avoid his assessing gaze.

"Sure," he said, and shrugged. After a moment, he asked, "Do you remember where the key is?"

There had been a couple of occasions when Jim had been very late at work and had called and asked me to go in and feed Archie his dinner and take him out to do his business. He had a key hidden in his backyard for just such a purpose.

We parted ways and I went back inside to have a shower and get ready for my next morning of surveillance.

GOOD-NATURED ARCHIE WAS PERFECTLY happy to climb into Loretta Jetta's passenger seat. He sat there panting slightly, staring out the windscreen, and, as far as I could tell, enjoying himself. Among the many amazing qualities dogs have, one of my favorites is that they are always up for an adventure. We drove west into Kitsilano.

I parked several blocks away from Chad's father's house. I got out of the car and went around to the passenger seat, took Archie's lead in hand, and beckoned him down. He shook himself happily, making his tags jingle, and I locked the car behind me.

The night before, I'd driven home from this very neighborhood with a racing heart, my mind whirling with thoughts. After getting over the initial shock of thinking that I'd found Emma, by the time I'd got home I'd nearly talked myself out of that idea.

"If Chad is a drug dealer, he likely always has security around him," I'd said to myself as I unlocked my front door.

But then I'd realized the guards weren't outside Chad's home in Yaletown. They were outside what I assumed was his father's home. How likely was it that that situation was normal? Not knowing any drug kingpins personally, I wasn't sure. But the security presence was the closest thing I had to a clue, so after making supper while arguing with myself, I decided to pursue it. That's when my Archie plan had fallen into place.

My idea was to be an innocent woman out walking her dog. I was disguised in case the people watching the house from the SUV out front happened to be the same fellows who had threatened me when Gray Suit had come to my house. I had borrowed a wig from Ellie and she had shown me how to put it on over my strawberry-blonde hair. It wasn't a perfect fit because we didn't have a skullcap, so, overtop of the wig, I was wearing my Vancouver Mounties baseball cap. I also dressed in a very large flannel shirt that I often wore when I was painting. Underneath that I had put on a puffer jacket, in hopes that I would look like I was a different size and shape than the person Gray Suit and his cronies had worked over.

It was raining, as usual, so I didn't have an excuse to wear sunglasses, but the day before I'd gone to a dollar store and picked up an inexpensive pair of reading glasses. When I got home, I'd been able to pop out the lenses; they weren't actually functional now, but they were large and had thick black frames with a cat-eye shape. Again I was hoping that they would alter my appearance just enough from how I'd looked the week before.

Archie and I approached the street from the west. We walked down the same side of the street as the house, and I worked really hard at my acting, pretending that I was just a neighbor out for a stroll with her dog. Archie gave an Oscar-worthy performance, pretending to be a dog out for a walk. The closer we got to the house, the faster my heart started to beat. By the time we were next door and Archie was sniffing the base of a maple tree, I was breathing with my mouth open from stress and tension. I praised Archie while he sniffed around the base of the tree because it actually gave me a moment to take surreptitious glances at the house.

I wasn't entirely sure what I wanted to accomplish by doing this, but one thing I knew was that more information was better than less. And this was the way that I had thought of to get a look at the house without being spotted. Hiding in plain sight, as it were.

Archie finished sniffing and we moved on down the side-walk. I could hear my heart beating in my ears, but I hoped my expression didn't convey my anxiety. I willed myself not to glance across the street at the large black SUV. My plan was to simply stroll by, glancing to my right, making note of anything I could see that was of interest, not having any idea what that might be.

Naturally, this was the moment when Archie decided to evacuate his bowels. As soon as we got to Chad's father's lawn, the dog started to display the quintessential body language that indicated that he had to poop.

"Not here, Archie," I whispered under my breath, giving a small tug at his leash. But once the process has begun, you can't stop it, as we all know.

Archie hunched his back and began to squeeze, a focused expression on his face. To prevent myself from panicking I tried to distract myself by digging around in my jeans pocket for a poop bag. Of course, I had to stand and wait until Archie had finished, which did give me a bit of an opportunity to look at the house. I made a mental note of the address with the intention of going back to City Hall and looking up its owner as well. I would have bet serious money that I would find this house was also owned by Claremont Holdings.

Archie completed his task and stepped forward, looking pleased with himself, and, like every suburban dog, he then stood patiently and waited for me to clean up after him. I stepped up onto the grass, flicking the poop bag open and pushing my right hand into it. I bent over and began the pinching motion of poop retrieval, thinking that maybe I was nearly home free.

The front door of the house opened. I glanced up, mid-scoop, and saw a woman closing the door behind her and coming down the two steps to the front walkway. She was dressed in a short leather jacket with a fur collar, skinny jeans, and black boots with stiletto heels. She had platinum blonde hair tied back in a ponytail and oversized gold hoop earrings that, to me, look ridiculous on everyone except JLo. I knew at a glance this was Chad's mother, given Laura's description. She came down the walkway giving me the hairy eyeball. As she passed by me, she said, "Make sure you get all of that. I'm tired of picking dog crap off my lawn."

"Absolutely," I said, without looking at her. I didn't want her to see my face.

Archie, everyone's friend, trotted toward her, wagging his tail. I had the leash wrapped around my left wrist and I was still bent over trying to pick up his poop. He strained at the end of the leash, trying to reach Chad's mom to say hello.

"Keep that thing away from me," she said.

Even though Archie hadn't got anywhere near her, she stepped sideways, making a wide circle around him. Then she crossed the sidewalk and the boulevard and stepped out onto the street and into a silver two-seater BMW. I kept my back to the road in case the men in the SUV were watching the exchange.

When I had scooped up all of Archie's poop, I stood and walked away from the house as innocently as possible, busying myself with tying a knot in the top of the poop bag. When we were a couple of houses away, I said to Archie, "You almost got us busted there, Mister."

At the sound of my voice, Archie turned and wagged and looked at me with a smiling face. The big goof.

WITH ARCHIE safely delivered back to Jim's house, I couldn't stop thinking about my exchange with Chad's mom on her front lawn. Now that I wasn't reacting and had calmed down slightly from my up-close-and-personal encounter, I had some time to think.

Something was nagging at me, tugging at the edge of my brain, but when I turned my thoughts toward it, it slipped away. I made a few notes in my notebook about what had happened but kept staring off into space, finding myself minutes later with my chin in my hand, not sure how long I had been in a trance. Whatever was irritating me was like when there's a tap dripping somewhere in the house but you can't figure out which faucet it is.

Notes done, I went up to my studio and tried to paint, but that wasn't happening either. I couldn't concentrate and found myself staring out into the backyard, thinking about Chad and Emma and Laura, and Chad's mom and dad. If Emma was being held at the house, I could totally see that Chad's mom and dad no doubt felt it was simply their right to have her with them. Given how Laura had described the family, I suspected that Emma was, to them, not a person but a possession, a way to wield their power over Laura rather than a young girl who needed her mom. If Emma was at the house, I hoped that they were treating her kindly and didn't have her chained in the basement. But no matter the circumstances, she still didn't belong there.

I absently swirled my paintbrush around in a jar of turpentine. After the drizzle that had been coming down all morning, the sun had started to come out. And because it was November and the sun was low in the sky, it came in through the windows and hit my napping couch square on. It was too tempting to resist, especially given the nights of poor sleep I'd been having. I glanced at the sunbeam and didn't have to think twice. I flopped down on the couch and snuggled into the warmth. I was asleep in about four seconds.

I HATE it when people tell me about their dreams. Dreams are so personal that the meaning only exists for the dreamer. I tend to have vivid dreams and usually remember them the next morning. I often dream of my sister, which inevitably leaves me with a bittersweet feeling when I wake up. And today during the nap that was exactly the case, except it felt like more like one of Blythe's visitations than a dream.

We were back at our high school, sitting on a stone wall that bordered one side of the property. We weren't supposed to sit on the wall, but we did anyway. Blythe was with her two closest girlfriends. In the dream I was almost on the outside, looking in at their interaction. They were dressed in the uniforms that we had worn; dark green kilts, white blouses, and dark green sweaters. As it was in real-life high school, all the girls wore their skirts as short as they were allowed to.

I was wearing the same uniform and was uncomfortably hot. I kept yanking at my sweater, trying to pull it up over my head, but it was like the sweater was too tight or my arms were too short. I couldn't get it off. It kept getting stuck around my shoulders. Blythe and her two friends were whispering and giggling about a secret. I felt left out, and between that and being uncomfortably warm trying to get the sweater off, I was frustrated.

Suddenly Blythe handed something to one of her friends, quickly and surreptitiously.

My eyes popped open. I didn't swim to the surface slowly. One minute I was deep in the dream and the next moment I was wide awake, lying on my couch. I was overly warm from the sun shining on me, which was undoubtedly why I had been struggling with my sweater in the dream.

But in that way that dreams only mean something to us personally, this one had answered the question that had been irritating me since I got home.

I had seen Chad's mother before.

And now I knew what I had to do next.

Chapter 26

The front door to the winemaking shop creaked open and I stepped from the watery November afternoon light into the reception room. I had gone to the back door of the building, but, unlike on my first visit, it had been locked. In here, the light was all artificial. I don't know how anybody can stand working in an environment like this day after day. I'd go mad. This time, I heard an electronic chime as I walked over the threshold, and shortly after I got to the counter the same young woman I'd seen on my last visit came through the doorway behind the counter and said hello.

It was the dream that had sent me over here. Blythe and her friend had been passing a joint between them, and in that weird way dreams do, that had made me realize that Chad's mother was the woman I'd seen on my first visit. She had been leaving, and I had caught a quick glimpse of her platinum hair and her leather jacket with the fur collar when Justin's mother had come into the growing room. I also remembered that I'd seen her silver BMW parked in the alley on that same day.

The young woman behind the counter looked at me with

a friendly expression. "Welcome back. How can we help you today?"

"I'd like to speak to Justin's mother, please." I felt a little goofy saying it that way, but I didn't know her name.

The young woman knew exactly who I was speaking of, and her expression closed down. "I'm afraid she's not here. Can I give her a message?"

I would have bet the deed on my house she was lying. I took one step closer to the counter and placed both hands on it, leaning forward and lowering my voice. "If Justin's mother doesn't come out here and talk to me in the next thirty seconds, I'm going to call 911, and within about four minutes there are going to be fourteen police cars outside. I'll tell them about the room at the back of the building. I'm sure they'll search it, and when they're done, they'll search every square inch of this place. And then, when they're done that, I'll suggest they get a forensic accountant involved, just to be sure all the books are above board." My tone was matter-of-fact. I wasn't trying to sound like Robert De Niro in a Martin Scorsese movie or anything, but she got the message.

She held my gaze for a few seconds and then spun around and disappeared through the doorway. She must have collided with Justin's mom, because almost immediately she came strutting into the reception area, puffed up like a rooster. She stood across the counter from me.

"Are you threatening me?" she said.

I touched the tip of one index finger to the side of my nose. "You got it in one, smarty."

She didn't like that. She straightened her spine and made herself taller. She opened her mouth, but I didn't let her speak.

"I want to speak to you privately. About Emma."

The cockiness in her eyes wavered ever so slightly. I had hit a nerve, and I felt a small victorious thrill run through me. The dream about Blythe hadn't been a guarantee. But as soon as the expression on Justin's mom's face changed, I knew I had interpreted it correctly. Hooray once more for my subconscious problem-solving.

Justin's mom stood quietly for a few seconds, clenching and unclenching her fists on the counter, which, on her side, was at waist height. Then she gave a slight jerk of her head and turned and walked back through the doorway from which she'd come. I followed her, and we went down a hallway and ended up in the same conference room where we'd met with Justin days earlier.

She closed the door behind me but didn't offer me a seat this time. She folded her arms across her chest and leaned against the wall beside the door, looking tough and indifferent. She didn't say a word, so I just started talking.

"You're friends with Lydia Allen, correct?"

She thought about this for a second and then nodded.

"And you know that the Allens have kidnapped their granddaughter, Emma, and are keeping her at their house in Kitsilano."

The muscles around her eyes shifted slightly but otherwise she didn't move.

"And it was you who tipped Chad off that I was here, looking for information about Emma."

Her face was still frozen. I decided to interpret her lack of denial as confirmation that I'd guessed correctly.

"So," I continued, "you're going to take me to Lydia's house and get me inside."

Finally she spoke. "Why would I do that?"

"So that I can see Emma for myself and let her mother know she's okay."

Her mouth curled up in an ugly smirk. "You can take my word for it. She's fine. Lydia loves that kid like crazy."

"I hate to break it to you, but your word isn't good enough for me. I need to see Emma for myself."

She pushed herself off the wall and stood with her legs

apart and her hands shoved in her jeans pockets. A very masculine pose. I was tired of thinking of her in my head as 'Justin's mom.'

"What's your name?" I said.

The unexpected question threw her. She screwed up her face. "What's it to you?"

I went over to the conference room door and opened it. Leaning out I yelled, "Hey!"

The girl from the reception desk appeared at the end of the hallway.

"Your boss, the one who's in here with me—what's her name?"

"Brittany, don't—" Justin's mom started to say.

"April. Why?" the girl said.

"Thanks, Brittany." I closed the door and stepped back. "So, April, we're going to go outside now and get in my car and go see Emma." I shifted the purse strap that was lying across my chest.

Her pose had changed again. Now she was leaning on the back of one of the chairs at the table. "As if," she said. It was like we were in junior high school.

"I think you heard what I said to young Brittany earlier. That was not an empty threat."

April made a scoffing noise. "Who cares? We have a license for the pot-growing operation."

"Mmmm," I said, affecting a casual tone. "And did you hear the bit about the forensic accountant? I'll bet if the VPD bean counters went over your books with a fine-toothed comb, they wouldn't like what they'd find."

"Pfffftt." She made a disparaging noise. "The cops can look all they like. Our books are clean."

She sounded confident. Her tone dared me to disagree. So much for that plan.

And then another thought occurred to me. "What if," I said, slowly and quietly, "I suggested to your boss, Chad, that he get *his* accountant to go over those same books extra carefully?"

The part about Chad being April's boss was a guess, but an educated one. The two families seemed to be intertwined. Chad was a drug kingpin, and April and her family were growing pot, at the very least. The part about her skimming funds from the business was a total guess, but I saw my comment hit a nerve. For the first time since we'd come into the room, April looked frightened. We stared at one another and I waited.

Finally, I heard her swear under her breath. The she said bitterly, "Fine. Let's get it over with."

"Attagirl." I opened the door and made a motion for her to lead the way.

"I have to get my purse," she said, trying to turn left.

"Nope." I used my body to guide her down the hallway toward the front of the store.

"I need to let my family know where I am," she said. "They won't know where I've gone."

"Well, then, they'll know how Emma's mom feels."

———————————————

Chapter 27

———————————————

I didn't waste any time getting to Chad's house. It took us about 25 minutes. It was Saturday, so Broadway was slightly less busy than it would have been during the week at this time. April sat silently beside me, brooding. I didn't really care. She was my way into the house. I wondered what would be my way out.

As I drove, I thought about who might be there. The guards would be outside, of course. Lydia and Emma would likely be inside. Would Chad himself be there? Or his dad? I had no way of knowing.

When we got nearly to the end of Broadway, I turned left onto Blenheim. We waited at the light on Tenth Avenue. My hands were gripping the steering wheel like it was a life ring and I was drowning. How had I gotten myself into this?

The light turned green and we drove south to 14th Avenue. I turned left again and prayed silently to the parking angels that I'd find a spot close to Chad's. The angels answered and gave me a spot in front of the house next door. When we passed the black SUV, which was parked facing the other direction, I willed myself not to look at the man in the driver's seat.

I turned the car off and unbuckled my seat belt. Then I turned to April. "Remember what I said. Get me into that house and keep your mouth shut, or I'll make sure Chad knows you've been ripping him off."

April glared at me but stayed silent. I wondered how long it had been since someone had bossed her around.

We got out of the car and approached the house through a drizzle that had started as we drove. I wiped my palms on my pants and tried to breathe.

Blythe appeared on my left. "What's your plan?"

"I don't have a plan."

April glanced at me, a confused expression on her face. "What did you say?"

"Nothing. Keep walking."

The three of us stayed quiet as we went up the steps to the front door. I pressed the doorbell and heard it make a deep 'ding-dong' sound inside the house.

Footsteps.

And then Lydia opened the door. "April! Hi, Doll. I didn't know you were coming over. Come in. Who's your friend?"

Lydia was all smiles. Her eyes flicked over me and I could see her trying to figure out where she knew me from.

"This is …" April started to say.

"Mary," I said, putting my hand out. "Nice to meet you."

The interior of the house was bright and light with pale laminate floors. I could see all the way to the kitchen at the back. A staircase to the second floor was to our left, and what seemed to be the dining room lay to our right.

"I was just about to make some coffee. Now I've got an excuse to get out some cookies as well." Lydia turned and clip-clopped down the hall toward the kitchen. She was wearing platform flip-flops, skinny jeans that looked like they were painted on, and a red V-neck sweater that was equally tight, making the very most of her abundant assets. Without the coat I'd first seen her in, she was tiny, just over five feet tall, I guessed, and maybe 110 pounds. But her boobs were over-sized and I suspected they were an after-market addition. Her platinum blonde hair looked stiff and fried at the ends, and it fell around her shoulders in oddly shaped waves. I wondered if some of it was a weave or extensions.

Lydia and April made small talk as they walked ahead of me. We entered the kitchen, which filled the back of the house and looked out onto the back yard. It too was bright, with windows and a sliding glass door lining the back wall. I glanced up and saw there was a skylight above as well. The cabinets were slightly darker than the floors, and the appli-ances were all stainless steel. It was sleek and modern and not at all what I expected. And there was no sign of Emma.

"Have a seat," Lydia said, pointing at the bar stools that were tucked under the kitchen counter. She began moving around, getting a bag of coffee grounds out of the freezer. Blythe was still with us, or rather me, but she had remained quiet since we'd come inside. She positioned herself in a 90-degree bend of the kitchen counter and watched Lydia. I was reassured by her presence but also wasn't paying too much attention to her. My nerves were jangling and my throat felt tight.

"I was telling Connie the other day—you know, Connie from the gym?" Lydia was talking to April and paying me no mind at all, which was more than fine with me. "I said to her… because you know she and her husband are getting divorced?"

"No!" April said, surprised.

"Yes! Did you know she caught him cheating on her? Okay, well, let me tell you *that* story first. It's a doozy."

While the coffee maker began making burbling noises, Lydia shook some store-bought cookies out of a bag onto a plate and placed them on the counter in front of April and me. We each took one. Lydia's long, purple nails with their squared-off ends made everything she did look awkward.

She prattled on about Connie and her cheating husband, hardly stopping to draw breath. She hadn't asked a single question about who I was or why we were there. April and I sat and listened to her, April occasionally interjecting a 'Really?' or a 'No way!'

The coffee maker grew quiet and, without breaking stride in her gossip narrative, Lydia poured us each a cup of coffee and put a bowl of sugar and a small waxed carton of milk on the counter in front of us.

I had stopped listening to Lydia's monologue and was wondering how to introduce the topic of Emma when I heard movement above our heads, coming from the second floor. A door closed and a few minutes later I heard the rushing water noises of a toilet flushing. My ears were straining to hear around Lydia's verbal diarrhea. I thought I caught the tread of feet on the stairs.

I leaned back slightly on my barstool so I could look back down the hallway toward the front of the house. Someone stepped off the bottom step, turned, and began walking toward us. She was thin and fragile looking, with a long dark braid lying over one shoulder and wearing an oversized sweatshirt that nearly swallowed her, jeans, and bare feet.

Emma.

Chapter 28

"Gramma, can I have something to eat?"

Emma came into the kitchen, barely giving April or me a glance. She stood at the end of the island, close enough that I could have reached out and touched her. Her shoulders were curled in on themselves and there were dark circles under her eyes that I didn't recall seeing in the photos Laura had shown me.

Lydia's expression changed. She glanced at Emma with irritation. "We just had lunch a few hours ago."

"But I'm hungry." Emma's voice was quiet but not whiny.

"Fine." Lydia made an impatient noise in the back of her throat. "There's some cheese in the fridge. Make yourself a plate of cheese and crackers and then go back upstairs and leave the grownups alone."

I tried to keep my eyes off Emma as she moved around the kitchen, getting herself a plate and then taking a box of crackers from the tall pantry beside the fridge. Lydia was still talking—would the woman ever shut up?—and April sat quietly, sipping her coffee and listening.

Emma put five or six crackers on the plate and then began to close the cracker box.

"Not *that* many!" Lydia snapped.

Emma took one cracker off the plate and put it back in the box.

Lydia rolled her eyes. "Don't blame me when you get fat," she said, and then continued the story she was telling April and me about the next-door neighbor who apparently had the temerity to want to paint the side of the fence they shared.

Crackers in place, Emma got a block of cheddar out of the fridge and took it to the counter opposite us. She reached for a cutting board, and then took a knife out of the block that was tucked into one corner. She cut herself some cheese slices and then reversed the process, putting everything away and wiping the knife off and drying it. She still hadn't looked at me the entire time she'd been in the room. I was trying to think of something to say to her but my brain seemed to have seized up.

And then she was gone. Without a word, she left the room and padded down the hallway. For an instant, I felt like I'd blown it.

I glanced across the room at Blythe and she was jerking her head toward Emma. "Go get her!"

I interrupted Lydia. "Is the powder room this way?"

Lydia's eyes swiveled to me and she nodded without pausing her story. I slid off the stool and followed in Emma's wake. Lydia wouldn't be able to see me from where she was standing, and April would only see me if she leaned back on her stool, like I had. I tiptoed as quickly as I could down the length of the hallway, and as I reached the bottom of the stairs, I saw that Emma was near the top.

I made the quietest noise I could and waved my arms above my head. Emma turned a few degrees and looked down at me, her expression flat. I flapped my hand in a 'come here' motion and crept up a few of the stairs, hoping she'd meet me in the middle. She didn't. She stood, frozen in place on the top stair.

As quietly as I could, I slithered up the rest of the stairs. When I was close enough, I whispered, "Emma, I'm a friend of your mom's. I'm here to take you home."

She looked at me skeptically. I imagined she wasn't all that trusting of adults these days, so I reiterated, "I promise you I'll take you to your mom."

Her expression didn't change, and she began to turn away from me.

As she stepped up onto the second-floor landing, I recalled the posters on her bedroom wall and whispered urgently, "*A deal is a promise and a promise is unbreakable.*" It was a quote from the *Wonder Woman* movie. I'd loved it, and so, it seemed, had Emma if the poster was any indication.

She turned back then, her eyes filling with tears. "Really? You'll take me to my mom?"

I nodded. "My car is out front. We can leave right now if we're quick."

Emma nodded, just a slight motion of her head, but it was enough for me.

I turned and began creeping back down the stairs. I could feel Emma following me. Then I heard a little click and nearly shrieked. But it was just Emma putting the cheese and cracker plate down on a stair behind her. My nerves were obviously shot. I thought I might never recover from this rescue mission. I wasn't feeling particularly Wonder Woman-ish, despite the quote.

Silently, we made our way toward the bottom of the stairs. I could hear Lydia in the kitchen, still talking. I gave a silent prayer for her fascination with herself. I felt something touch my back and realized it was Emma, holding onto a fold in my jacket.

I reached the bottom step. The front door was about four feet away, on the other side of the small tiled foyer. Three quick steps and we'd be out the door and gone. I paused and turned around to face Emma. Then I leaned in closer and whispered in her ear, "My car is dark blue. It's parked up the street a bit that way." I pointed in the direction of the car. "The doors are unlocked." I could feel her nodding, stray hairs that had come out of her braid tickling my face. "When we get out that front door, you are going to run as fast as you can and get in the passenger seat." I pulled back and looked into her eyes. Emma nodded again, her expression grim and serious. I gave her a thumbs up and turned back toward the door. Lydia's monologue continued in the kitchen. My foot moved down off the last stair riser and I took a deep breath.

Then the front door swung open toward me and there was a man filling the frame.

Chapter 29

I had never seen this man before, but I recognized him immediately. He was beefy, clearly someone who liked lifting weights, but he was also dressed in a suit that fit him so well it had to be handmade, just like Gray Suit's. I bet they had the same tailor. This suit was dark with a fine pinstripe, the tie at his throat a bronze color. His hair was brown, thick, and cropped short, and his chin, jaw, and upper lip had a fashionable layer of stubble.

Chad.

His eyes darted from me to Emma and then back to me again. "Who the hell are you?"

Before I could answer, Lydia came out of the kitchen and down the hallway toward us, holding her coffee cup. "Hello, Cookie. You're home early."

No matter how big and tough and bad-ass the man, his mom could still call him a silly nickname.

He didn't answer her. "Who is this?" he said, pointing at me.

Lydia glanced at me. "This is, uh, a friend of April's." She had forgotten the name I'd given her. "They popped in for a cup of coffee."

Chad's eyes flicked from his mom, to me, to Emma, and then back to his mom. He obviously had good instincts, and something wasn't sitting right with him. I stayed quiet and relied on social convention to protect me for as long as it could.

Lydia, god bless her, was oblivious. "Are you hungry? Let me make you something."

Chad's shoulders dropped fractionally. "No, I just came to grab a file from the office that I forgot this morning."

As Chad began to close the door behind him, I noticed a bodyguard-type guy standing outside on the front walkway, holding a black umbrella over his head.

We were five people crowded into a relatively small space, and Chad took up much of that space with his height, bulk, and energy. I threw a glance at April and willed her to silence.

Chad looked at Emma as the door closed. "You shouldn't be out here. Go to your room." The directive was quiet but filled with menace.

I couldn't see Emma because she was directly behind me. I waited for her to move, but she didn't. Her father took two steps toward us, aiming for the staircase. I moved to my right, starting to let him pass, my mind whirling with options about what to do now. He seemed to be going upstairs. Should I wait until he was out of sight and then grab Emma and make a break for it?

He stepped past me and crushed that plan in its infancy by taking Emma by the elbow and beginning to lead her up the stairs.

I thought about screaming. I thought about pulling out my phone and dialing 911. I thought about pretending to have a seizure so that attention would be diverted away from Emma and maybe she'd have the presence of mind to run. Then I thought of the bodyguard outside and flushed that idea.

Everything was happening so quickly. Chad had been

inside the house for a maximum of 90 seconds and yet the tension and stress inside me had made it feel like years.

The 911 call seemed to be my best bet. I reached into my purse and began feeling around for my phone.

Suddenly, Emma's hand flashed over the banister and grabbed her grandmother's coffee cup. Lydia made a little beep of surprise. In one movement, Emma pivoted and flung the coffee directly into her father's eyes.

Chad roared and let go of her elbow, hands rushing to his face. Emma turned again, and before she could take one step I was at the front door, pulling it open. The girl zipped past me and we both skipped the stairs and simply leapt off the low front stoop onto the grass.

Behind us, inside the house, I could hear Chad screaming and then a crash and a high-pitched yelp. I wondered if he had slipped in the coffee on the stairs and fallen. I wasted no more time thinking about it.

Emma and I shot past the bodyguard, who was facing the other direction. I saw him turn and belatedly realize he was witnessing an escape.

Emma reached Loretta Jetta before I did and pulled open the passenger door. Without looking to see if there were cars coming, I ran out onto the street and yanked open the driver's door. I had left the key in the ignition and was turning it before my bum had settled on the seat. Emma was beside me, pulling her door closed. I didn't even worry about mine.

I turned the key.

Loretta fired up on the first try.

I threw her into drive, jerked the wheel to the left, and pulled away, scraping the bumper of the car ahead of me. The momentum of the car closed my door for me, and I floored the gas pedal and drove at an exceptionally unsafe speed down the residential street.

I took a quick glance in the rearview mirror and could see the bodyguard running for his vehicle, which I was very glad was parked facing the other direction. He'd have to go around the block to come back in the direction I was going, which would slow him down. Chad was standing on the front lawn, one hand to his face, the other waving around wildly. I imagined the air was blue around him.

At the fourth cross street—I'd sped through the first three without even looking for crossing traffic—I turned right and headed over to 16th Avenue. My plan was to zig and zag and disappear as quickly as possible.

I glanced over at Emma. She was panting and her face was red, her eyes wide and staring ahead. She felt my gaze and turned her head to look at me. I grinned at her. For a split second she held my eyes. And then she grinned back.

"Amazing job, Diana of Themyscria," I said.

Her grin spread wider.

"Put your seatbelt on," I said.

She rolled her eyes at me, smiling, and did as I asked.

WHILE EMMA and I took a very indirect route east through town, I got her to reach into my purse, which was still strapped around my torso, and find my phone. Together we got it unlocked with my thumb print and then I got Emma to find Ellie's number.

"Go ahead. Dial," I said, glancing at Emma.

She pressed the number and waited while the phone rang.

"Put it on speaker," I said, and she did.

Ellie's voice came on the line. "Where are you?" she said, without preamble.

I glanced at Emma and nodded.

"Hi Ellie," Emma said quietly into the phone.

Ellie's shriek filled the car. Emma laughed and smiled at the phone.

"Is that you, baby girl?"

"It is," Emma said.

"Sweet suffering saints and angels. I can't believe it." I could hear Ellie sniffling.

"Listen, Ellie," I said, "we've got cause for celebration but we'll need to do that later."

I could hear noises in the background and then the sound of Ellie blowing her nose.

I gave her a moment and then said, "Are you listening?" while simultaneously choking up, smiling at Emma, and running a yellow light at 25th and Oak.

"Give me one blessed second, honey." She honked again. "Okay. Now I'm listening."

I could still hear her sniffling but I gave her instructions anyway while Emma held the phone out toward me. "You need to get over to Laura's ASAP. We're just crossing Cambie street so we'll be there in fifteen minutes or so." I continued talking and driving, giving Ellie instructions, Emma holding the phone.

THE REUNION WAS MOVING but very short-lived. I gave Laura and Emma thirty seconds to reunite. Ellie was whizzing around the apartment, pushing clothes and shoes into two of those enormous blue Ikea reusable bags. I couldn't believe she'd thought to bring them with her. Before we arrived, she had already filled a third one with Emma's clothes. I could see the bedraggled teddy bear poking out between two sweaters.

I stood by the sliding glass doors at the front of the room, watching the street, while Ellie helped Laura and Emma pack. No one spoke. I glanced over and saw Emma coming out of her room stuffing books into a backpack. When I looked back outside there was a large, black SUV crawling down the street toward Laura's building.

"That's it," I said. "We have to go."

Laura began to object and I was about to argue with her. But then Emma walked over and took her by the elbow. "Come on, Mom. It's just stuff. We can replace it."

Laura gave one last pitiful glance around the living room and then followed as her daughter led her toward the front hall.

The four of us trotted down the stairs, single file, Ellie at the front and me bringing up the rear. Loretta Jetta was parked directly in front of the building: the parking angels were still looking out for us. I glanced left and right through the glass front door of the building, but didn't see the SUV. I dashed out of the building, threw myself into Loretta's driver's seat and started her up. This time she gave me some trouble, as if to remind me not to rest on my laurels. When the engine fired after three tries, I pulled out of the parking space.

I zipped down the street, passing the parked cars on either side, and glancing in my mirrors every five seconds. So far, no sign of the black SUV. Maybe it hadn't been Chad's henchmen after all.

I drove east for three blocks and still there was no sign that I was being followed. I let out a huge breath. "We did it!"

I signaled and turned right onto a street that would lead me up to Broadway. And then slammed on the brakes. Stopped in the road and blocking my path was a black SUV.

The passenger door opened and Chad stepped out onto the road.

———————————————

Chapter 30

———————————————

I put Loretta in reverse and looked over my shoulder so I could start to back up. Another black SUV pulled around the corner and stopped behind me. I sighed and shifted into park.

Chad left his passenger door open and walked toward my car, his impeccable suit—even with the coffee stains on the lapels—making him appear no less threatening. He approached the driver's door and leaned down to look through the window at me. His eyes were bloodshot and the skin around them was tight and inflamed. His glance swept the inside of Loretta Jetta, and his expression went from furious to apocalyptic in 0.7 seconds.

His dark eyes came back and met mine. "Where is she?"

I hadn't rolled down the window—duh—so we were speaking to each other through the glass.

"Aloe vera," I said.

"What?"

"If you put some aloe vera on that burn, it will help it to heal."

He shook his head like an angry bull shaking off a fly. "Where is my daughter?"

I did an exaggerated glance around the inside of the car, which was empty, and then looked back at him. I gave an exaggerated shrug, lifting my palms in the air.

The parts of his face that weren't burned started to color. I could see the flush rising up from where his shirt collar met his neck, flowing over his chin, then his cheeks, and on up to his forehead.

"Have you had your blood pressure checked lately?" I said. "It's the silent killer, you know, and you look like you're experiencing some stress."

He stood up now and his head disappeared from my view. I took the opportunity to reach into my purse and pull out my phone.

The driver of the SUV in front of me climbed out and started approaching on Loretta's passenger side.

Chad's face reappeared at my window, his reddened eyes shooting darts. His voice was low and even, but I heard it clearly. "If you don't tell me where Emma is in the next ten seconds…"

I glanced to my right, where the SUV driver/bodyguard was now glowering at me through that window. He was all dressed in black and was a bulked-up version of Chad, which was saying something. He started aggressively yet rhythmically tapping on the window with a knuckle.

I had the phone to my ear. "Police, fire or ambulance?" the voice on the phone asked.

"Police, please," I said, turning back to look at Chad. Our faces were mere inches apart with just the glass between us, and no doubt he could punch through that if he chose to.

A different voice came through the phone. "Police. What's your emergency?"

Still holding Chad's eyes I said, "I'd like to report a traffic violation."

"What's your location?" the voice said.

"I'm on Windsor Street, just south of Eighth Avenue."

Chad straightened up. He hesitated, and then walked back to the vehicle he'd gotten out of. His goon followed him.

"My mistake," I said to the 911 operator. "I don't think I'll need your help today."

Just before Chad climbed into his SUV, he turned and looked back through Loretta's windshield at me.

"This isn't over," he said, voice raised so I could hear him.

I stuck my tongue out at him.

Chapter 31

While I was being the decoy, distracting Chad and his henchmen, Ellie, Laura, and Emma had gone out of the apartment building via a little-used back door. Ellie had parked illegally in the alley, and they had managed to escape, going west, while I was drawing the goons eastward.

Ellie took Laura and Emma to Mack and John's, where they stayed for two nights. I had called ahead, briefly explaining the situation to the two men. It was a testament to both their characters and their kindness that they agreed at once to house two strangers at a moment's notice. I had never been more grateful to call Mack and John my friends.

Laura, however, had objected to this idea, naturally, given Mack's job. Standing in Mack and John's front hallway with one hand on the front doorknob, seconds from fleeing, she had explained that the police had been almost no help when she was married to Chad and was being assaulted almost daily. They had diminished her experience and referred to Chad's violence as 'misunderstandings.' Eventually she had figured out that they were in Chad's pocket. But the damage was done, and she had not trusted any officer of the law since.

We had reasoned with her and tried to cajole her, to little effect. Eventually it was Emma who convinced her to stay.

"I'm exhausted, Mom," she said. "I just want to lie down."

Laura had relented, but even though Mack was a gentle and genial host, she never warmed up to him.

ON THE SECOND DAY, I dropped over to see how things were going. Emma and Laura were quiet while we all ate lunch. Mack and I regaled them with tales from our childhood, trying to lighten the mood. Laura responded with polite smiles, but Emma wasn't engaged at all. It seemed that when the adrenaline from our Great Escape had faded, so had some of the strength and chutzpah she'd exhibited. Mack said she clung to her mother, rarely letting Laura out of her sight. She seldom spoke and seemed to try to take up as little space in the house as possible, a mouse sneaking around, tucked against the baseboards.

After lunch, Mack and I were cleaning the kitchen while Emma and Laura put a puzzle together on the dining room table. Well, in actuality, Emma worked on the puzzle and Laura gazed at her, occasionally touching her hair and stroking her back.

I was wiping down the island when I said, "I'm sorry I didn't tell you what's been going on the last couple of weeks."

He looked up from the sink. "Yeah. What's up with that?"

"Laura was really adamant she didn't want the police involved."

"I'm not 'the police'," he said, putting air quotes around the last two words. "I'm your friend first."

"I know that. But Laura didn't know you, and I felt I needed to keep her trust. If it had gone on for much longer, I would have got you involved."

He nodded, and I could see him thinking. "Chad Allen is known to us."

Now it was my turn to nod.

Mack continued. "I'm concerned that you've pissed him off."

"You and me both."

My phone rang. I didn't recognize the number, but I knew who it would be: a woman named Suzanne from the underground network. She was calling me because we'd destroyed Laura's cell phone before we left her apartment. Chad still had Emma's phone, of course, and we couldn't take a chance that he'd trace Laura's.

"Hello?" I said into the phone while digging in my purse for my notebook.

Suzanne skipped any preliminaries and gave me the information we'd been waiting for. I took thorough notes while Mack dried a copper saucepan, watching me. When I hung up ten minutes later, I took a deep breath.

"Are they all set?" Mack asked.

I nodded.

"When do they leave?"

"Tomorrow. Early."

I stood up and went into the dining room and took a seat at the table. Emma was concentrating deeply and didn't look up. Laura met my eyes and must have read something there. "Was that Suzanne?"

"Yes."

Laura sat up straighter, steeling herself. She looked at her daughter. "Emma, honey. We need to listen to what Freddie's going to tell us."

Emma glanced up at me and dropped her hands into her lap. "We're leaving, aren't we?"

I nodded and Emma started to cry. These were the first tears I'd seen from her since I'd found her at Lydia's house.

Her chin quivered slightly. She tipped sideways and put her face on her mom's shoulder. Laura stroked her back.

"I want to see Olivia," Emma said, her voice slightly muffled. "I need to say goodbye."

My heart broke for her.

Laura spoke quietly. "I'm so sorry, honey. It's just not safe."

Emma sat up and wiped her cheeks on her sleeves. "But she'll be worried about me."

"You're right. She will be. She cares about you. But we can't risk it, sweetheart. Your dad knows too much about our life now. I'm certain he's got people watching Olivia's house."

Emma made a growling noise of frustration in her throat. "It's not *fair*!" She stood up from the table abruptly, pushing her chair back, and stomped out of the room. We listened to her heavy footsteps on the stairs and then the slam of the bedroom door.

Emma had been so brave, and, in the end, she had rescued herself. But there are limits to what any thirteen-year-old can take, and it appeared Emma was hitting that wall.

Laura sighed and dropped her chin to her chest.

"It's for her own safety," I said, lamely.

"I know," Laura said. "It's just. . . I wonder about the damage all this is doing to her."

I thought about this. "It's doing some, no doubt about it."

"Thanks for that," Laura said, but without bitterness. It was the closest I'd heard her coming to making a joke since I'd met her.

"There's no getting around it, unfortunately. But what's the alternative? You stayed with Chad all those years ago and Emma saw you get the crap beaten out of you on the regular."

Laura sighed.

I continued. "This way, she'll be safe and you'll be safe. She might not realize it now, but what you're modeling to her is an unwillingness to be the victim. She'll see that eventually, even if she can't see it now."

"I hope you're right." She leaned back in her chair and dug around in her jeans pocket. Pulling out a tissue, she wiped her eyes and then looked at me, resigned. "What did Suzanne say?"

"You guys are booked on a flight tomorrow from Abbotsford Airport."

"Abbotsford? Why there?"

"She thinks there's less likelihood that Chad will have people watching it than the Vancouver airport."

Laura nodded. "Where are we going?"

"I don't know. Suzanne said the fewer people who know the details, the better. I'll drive you guys out there in the morning and she'll meet you there with new ID and get you on the flight."

She gave a weary sigh. "More new names. Emma won't like that. She doesn't remember when her name changed the first time." She thought for a few seconds. "Will someone let the library know? And my landlord?"

I nodded. "Suzanne's going to take care of that. Much of the stuff at your apartment will be donated to the shelter so other women who are in similar situations can use it."

"That's something, at least."

It was all hard. And shitty. There was nothing I could say to Laura that would make it any less so. So I just sat with her in silence.

Chapter 32

The early Christmas lights had started to appear on residential houses and in shop windows. It wouldn't be December for another week, but some folks like to get a jump on the festive season. I had stopped decorating when my parents moved to the alpaca farm. I tended to go up and spend a few days with them over the holiday week and couldn't see the point of decorating my house if I was the only person who saw it.

Ellie, on the other hand, looked for any excuse to doll up both herself and her laneway house. As I walked across the lawn from my back door to her front door, with a bottle of wine tucked against me, I could see her inside, standing on a stool, stringing a set of lights around the sliding glass doors that led onto her patio. A ceramic Rudolph with a light-up red nose and a small tree with branches made entirely of tiny white lights had joined the other statutes, figurines, and plant pots on the little patio. Soon there wouldn't be room for Ellie out there, let alone a guest.

I let myself in and set the wine on the kitchen island.

Ellie glanced over her shoulder. "How does that look?"

She was almost tall enough to be doing the job without the stool.

"It's drooping a bit in the middle."

"Just like me, honey." She made an adjustment and then stepped back to look at her handiwork, nodding with satisfaction.

The patio wasn't the only thing getting decked out. There were other strings of lights draped along the walls and over the kitchen cabinets. Red and green candles were positioned just so on tables and on top of a small bookshelf. Two houses from a ceramic village nearly filled the coffee table. And a small reusable Christmas tree took pride of place in a corner. It was covered with so many decorations, silver garlands, icicles, lights, and other doo-dads that it looked like the North Pole had thrown up on it.

"Nog?" Ellie asked, sashaying over to the fridge.

"No thanks. I'll stick to wine."

She was wearing a sleeveless, red silk dress in the 'fit and flare' shape of a 1950s hostess, complete with petticoat under the skirt, and she looked fabulous. I told her so.

"Thank you, honey." She paused briefly, posing for me. "It's new. Do you like it?"

"Very much. Is there someone special coming to the party tonight?"

"Maybe more than one someone special." She winked at me while she poured some eggnog into a small tumbler and added a liberal portion of rum.

It was an annual tradition in the Ellie Spenser household that the Christmas season got kicked off nice and early with her seasonal party. Her partners and colleagues from the hair salon she co-owned would be coming, along with friends and even some clients she was close to. I would stay for the first hour or so and then make a quiet exit. Since Blythe died, the holidays weren't the same for me.

Ellie sipped her nog and took a look around the room.

Seeming satisfied, she put her glass down and trained her gaze on me. "Now," she said, "tell me how you're doing. You look tired."

It was slightly less than a week ago that Ellie and I had driven Laura and Emma out to the Abbotsford airport long before dawn on a freezing morning. After I had told Laura and Emma about the plans to spirit them away, I'd left them at Mack's and gone downtown and bought two large suitcases and one carry-on. They'd spent that afternoon and evening quietly packing what little they had. The meal John had made that night was glorious, but we were all in too somber a mood to really enjoy it.

When Ellie and I had handed Laura and Emma off to Suzanne in the airport, Emma started to walk away and then suddenly rushed back and threw her arms around me.

"A deal is a promise, and a promise is unbreakable," she had whispered into my chest.

I had choked up and started to say something, but she broke away and walked back to her mom and Suzanne. Laura waved to us, sadly, and mouthed, "Thanks".

And then they were gone, wheeling their unscuffed suitcases around a corner and out of sight.

Ellie had wrapped a long arm around my shoulders and leaned her head onto the top of mine. We'd stood there for several minutes, sniffling, until finally she'd straightened up and said, "I need a drink."

It was 6:10 AM.

"Me too," I said.

In the ensuing few days, I'd drifted around my house, trying and failing to paint, and napping a lot. But Ellie was right. Despite the naps, I was tired. I took a sip of wine and smiled weakly at her.

"It's an amazing thing you did," she said.

"We both did it."

"Not really. I got the ball rolling, but you took it over the goal line."

I smiled. "A sports metaphor? In that dress?"

She shrugged and took another sip of nog. "Old habits."

"I just hope they're safe now and that Chad never finds them."

"He won't."

I voiced the thing that had been weighing on me. "Men like Chad hate to lose. It isn't about Emma at all. He doesn't really care about her. He'll just be pissed that he lost that battle. She's a possession and he lost control of her."

Ellie nodded.

"And that could make him persistent and extra dangerous." My stomach tightened at the thought.

"We have to trust that Suzanne and her network know what they're doing."

I took another sip of wine. She was right. But it was hard not to worry.

My house was being watched; I knew that for sure. Several times in the past few days I'd seen a black SUV with tinted windows crawling down my street. And twice I'd come home to find my mail lying wet on my front steps. I had a mailbox, as most houses do, that was attached to the house beside my front door. Someone was clearly going through the mail, looking for contact from Emma and Laura. I'd phoned Suzanne the first time it happened and asked her to pass a message to them, telling them under no circumstances to mail me anything. She said they knew that rule, but when I told her what had happened, she promised to reinforce it with them.

"Have you ever been abused?" I asked Ellie.

She stood up to her full height and held her hands out in a gesture that said, *Are you kidding? Look at me.* "Having been born in a man's body, I have the advantage of height and strength. No one would dare. What about you?" she asked.

I thought back. "No. Never physically abused. But I had a

boyfriend in university who was really controlling. What was scary was how quickly I slipped into trying to please him. Making myself smaller and walking on eggshells around him." I shivered at the memory.

"What happened?"

I snorted. "Thankfully, he dumped me at brunch one Sunday. In front of three other people."

"So he was a real class act."

"Yup," I said.

"Good riddance." Ellie raised her glass and we clinked.

"After that, it took me a while before I trusted myself again."

"I bet."

I paused, thinking. "I know that's not nearly the same thing as what Laura's been through, but that experience helped me understand why she stayed with Chad and tried to make it work in the early days. And how much courage it took her to leave."

There was a knock at Ellie's door. Her guests were arriving.

"Come in!" she yelled, and then, putting one large hand over mine, she said, "From the bottom of my heart, thank you for helping them. You put yourself in danger, and I will never forget it."

We held each other's eyes for a moment. "It was my honor."

Chapter 33

I loved school. I loved the social aspect particularly, but I also loved the learning. Every August, I was so excited to go back and see my friends and learn more.

Not everyone feels this way, of course. As I sat in Loretta Jetta outside Emma's school, I watched the tweens mill about in the schoolyard and felt like I could pick out the ones who were keen to learn, those who were indifferent, and those who would rather be anywhere else. They were noisy, as only preteens can be, with exaggerated gestures and dramatic facial expressions. I wondered what it would be like to have one or two of these creatures under one's own roof.

Loud, I imagined. And messy.

Blythe appeared beside me. "But you never really wanted kids of your own."

"I know. I was just wondering what it would be like."

"You would have been a fabulous mom. And an amazing aunt for Pickle."

We were both staring forward, watching the schoolyard. I didn't answer, but I agreed with her—about the aunt thing, at least. I would have been the coolest aunt ever, teaching Pickle about art and travel and how to find a pair of shoes that are both dressy and comfortable.

Without looking at me, Blythe spoke again. "You done good, little sister. Emma and Laura are safe because of you."

"And now I've got a drug lord who hates me."

"He'll get over it."

I turned to her for the first time since she'd appeared. "Will he? I'm not sure about that. I feel like grudges are what keep drug lords motivated."

Out of the passenger window I spotted what I'd been waiting for. Without waiting for Blythe's reply, I jumped out the car and ran around to the sidewalk.

Olivia was walking toward the schoolyard gate, reading a book, as she had been the first day I'd followed her. She must have heard me approach and looked up.

"Hi, Olivia."

"Hi." Her expression was unreadable. When we'd first met, I'd thought she was hiding her feelings from me, but I was starting to think that was just her natural expression. Neutral. Unamused.

I bent sideways slightly. "What are you reading today?"

She held the book so I could see the cover. "*Beautiful Joe*," I said. "A Canadian classic."

"I've read it before, of course," she said with a slightly defensive tone. "But I like the theme of caring for all creatures. And how it explores the start of the Industrial Age."

Jeez. This kid was wasted on grade eight. She needed a professorship at the very least.

"Plus, I like dogs," she continued. "My mom won't let us have a dog."

"I have another book for you." I reached into my bag and pulled out a thick paperback. I held the book up facing her.

She read the title. "*Lorna Doone.*"

"Have you read it?"

She shook her head.

"It's a good one. It was my grandfather's favorite book. It's meaty, but I know you'll manage."

"I read all the Harry Potter books in three weeks," she said proudly, and then added, "when I was eight."

"You won't have any trouble with this one, then." I handed it to her. "And if you look inside, there's something in there, just for you."

She tucked *Beautiful Joe* under one arm so she could leaf through *Lorna Doone*. The book opened in the middle, revealing a folded sheet of paper.

"What's this?" she said, unfolding it. She started reading and then looked up at me. "It's from Emma."

I nodded. "She hated that she had to leave without saying goodbye to you. So she asked me to deliver this."

For the first time since I'd met her, emotion flitted across Olivia's face. She folded the letter up again quickly and tucked it back into the book. "I'll save it for later," she said. I thought that was going to be all, but, while busying herself with tucking both books into her backpack, she said, "I miss her."

"I know she misses you too."

The school bell shrieked.

Emotions under control, Olivia put the straps of the backpack on her shoulders once more. "Goodbye," she said, and walked away.

"See ya," I said, but I doubted she heard me.

"That is one stoic kid," Blythe said, now standing at my shoulder. "She remind you of anyone?"

I turned to look at her. "No. Who?"

She looked incredulous. "You! The reading obsession. The love for school when the rest of us hated it."

"Really?" I screwed my face up at her. "Was I that controlled with my emotions?"

We turned and began walking back toward my car. "Well, no. That's one area where you guys differ. You were all over the map. A 'large emotional landscape,' as Mom used to say."

I tried defending myself. "Feelings are big when you're thirteen."

"And fourteen, and fifteen…" Blythe said, grinning slyly.

We climbed into Loretta Jetta and teased each other all the way home. Just as we'd done when we were young. And both of us were alive.

the end

Author's Note

The most dangerous place for a woman is often her home.

While *Lark Underground* is a work of fiction, it was inspired by a story I heard about a woman and her daughter who lived 'underground' with fake identities for years, trying to escape an abusive husband and father.

That story stayed with me, and I wanted to explore it in a way that gave power back to the mother and the daughter. That was the genesis of the idea for *Lark Underground*. While we can't always create a satisfying resolution in every life situation, we can do it in fiction.

Another reason this story is close to my heart is that I was involved in a cult for ten years in the 1990s. (Yes, really. You can read about that in my award-winning memoir, *Cult, A Love Story*.) The dynamic that exists in cults is essentially the same as the one that exists in an abusive domestic relationship. The only difference is that in a cult, the relationship is one-to-many (the guru to their disciples), and in a spousal relationship it's one-to-one. As a result of my cult experience, I can completely empathize with Laura. Perhaps this novel is one way for me to take back power for myself after that cult experience as well.

If you or someone you know is experiencing domestic violence, I encourage you to reach out for help. You are not alone, and there are people who have been where you are and can help you climb out of that situation.

I know with 100 percent certainty, and from personal experience, that you are both enormously resilient and worthy of genuine love. And even if you're not sure of these things yourself at this moment, that does not mean they are not true.

In Canada: ShelterSafe
www.sheltersafe.ca

In the US: The National Domestic Violence Hotline.
www.thehotline.org or 1-800-799-7233

In the UK: Refuge for Women and Children.
www.nationaldahelpline.org.uk or 0808-2000-247

Acknowledgments

Many thanks to my peeps on Facebook who answer my random questions about everything from coffee habits to the names for pots and pans.

Special thanks to Dean Hamilton, Annabel Melnyk, and Maggie Rayner for their descriptions of the interior of a Vancouver Special.

Bob Sirrine is a thorough and keen proofreader and I appreciate him so much. Thank you, Bob!

Also by Alexandra Amor

Freddie Lark Mysteries

Lark Lost

Historical Mysteries

Charlie Horse

Horse With No Name

The Outside of a Horse

Water Horse

The Horse You Rode In On

A One Horse Open Sleigh

Juliet Island Romantic Mysteries

Love and Death at the Inn

Children's Animal Adventure Novels

Sugar & Clive and the Circus Bear

Sugar & Clive and the Bank Robbery

Sugar & Clive and the Movie Star

Larry at the Wedding (A Sugar & Clive Novella)

Memoir

Cult, A Love Story

About the Author

Alexandra Amor writes books about love, connection, and the search for understanding.

Alexandra began her writing career with an award-winning memoir about ten years she spent in a cult in the 1990s. She has written four animal adventures for middle-grade readers, several historical mysteries set in 1890 in frontier British Columbia, two private investigator mysteries set in Vancouver, and a cozy romantic mystery.

A former Vancouverite, Alexandra now lives in a magical fishing village on Vancouver Island and spends each day writing and creating. When she's not doing that you'll likely find her walking on a beach or worrying that the vacuum cleaner feels ignored. In her spare time she serves on the board of her local hospice association.

Learn more at AlexandraAmor.com

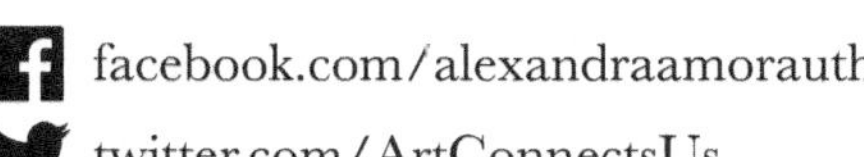

facebook.com/alexandraamorauthor

twitter.com/ArtConnectsUs

instagram.com/alexandraamorauthor

9 781988 924274